GIVE ME
A
Reason

TIA MCCOLLORS

ISBN-13: 978-0692401583 (Thoughts In Action, LLC)
ISBN-10: 069240158X

Give Me A Reason

www.TiaMcCollors.com
Tia@TiaMcCollors.com

Thoughts In Action, LLC

Dedication

For my cousin, Kiysha
Now you can stop asking me to put your name in a book!

Chapter 1

I sat on the patio of my third floor condo and watched the tender exchange between the couple below. As he embraced her, his chin rested in her thick, black hair. She nuzzled her head against his chest. I'd seen them plenty of times and they were always stuck together like Velcro. By the pool. Cornered together in the elevator. They lived in their world of love. I could also tell they were young. They didn't know any better.

He playfully pinned his woman against a silver sports car, sleek and shiny as a bullet. She yielded to his touch as he kissed her on the bridge of her nose, let his lips run down to hers, then down to her neck. She melted. Heck, I melted. I drained my glass of the last swallow of the freshly squeezed lemonade I'd made that morning and went back inside. Show's over.

As if that wasn't enough, another heated love scene from a movie taunted me in high definition from my flat screen television mounted over the fireplace. The muted volume silenced the man and woman's words but I could tell she was clinging to every word he said. Hidden beneath his promises, there were probably lies. Television or reality, that's usually how it went. I'd once been a hopeless romantic, but somewhere between broken promises, a broken engagement, and a broken heart, that had changed. They always say when love calls you better answer. I say, let it go to voicemail.

I picked up the remote and powered off the television. Enough of that, too.

I breathed in deeply and inhaled love. My kind of love. It was love in the form of red velvet cupcakes with only seven more minutes before I slid them from the oven and topped them with my special cream cheese frosting. I fell back onto the oversized pillows of my sofa, and grabbed the top magazine off the stack of house decorating and renovation magazines that I subscribed to. Two things always put me in good spirits: baking and anything related to real estate. I specialized in luxurious desserts and even more luxurious homes.

I lived in a 1,256 square feet condo by choice because as a single entrepreneur, I preferred to have my amenities at my fingertips in my life-work-play community. I could easily have my dry cleaning picked up if I was too busy to drop it off myself, could request housecleaning services when I wanted the white glove treatment, and at my mother's insistence, I resided in a secured community.

The only thing it lacked was the kitchen of my dreams. One day I'd have my restaurant-style ranges and cooktops, double ovens, deep stylish sinks and those hands-free faucets. I was easy to please. With one swipe in front of the sensor I could rinse icky egg yolks, cream cheese, or flour off my hands without leaving residue on the handles. For now, however, I was content in the perfect pad for a woman with big dreams.

Dreams take time, but lately my mother hadn't been as patient about my climbing the ladder of success.

"Vaughn," she said, "you need to think about more than your career. You need to think about getting married and having children. Those awards and magazine articles aren't going to take care of you when you get old. I know there have got to be some good men in Atlanta. Everybody can't be like those crazy reality shows. If that's what the men are like there, you need to move back to Denver."

I didn't care how much Meta Holiday-Simms whined. I wasn't moving back to Denver and she knew it. I loved my mother as much as I loved myself, but the 1400 miles between us was the best thing for our relationship. She could force her advice on me, and I could choose what I wanted to ignore.

I gave my mother the same spiel every time.

"If a man truly wants to be with me, he'll be up for the chase. However long it takes."

"Then slow down because you're moving too fast.

How can a man catch up with you when you're always on the go? I know who *will* run after you. Trace. Trace is ready for the chase. You better open your eyes before he takes off running after somebody else."

In my mother's eyes, Trace Moseley might as well have been Jesus' brother. She'd thought the same thing about Roderick and neither one of us would've suspected that he'd confess his wrongdoings two months before our vows. And neither one of us would've suspected that less than six months later he'd say "I do" to another woman. I wasn't sure if I could trust my judgment or my mother's judgment anymore when it came to matters of love.

"A man likes to know a woman is taking care of her business," I reminded her. "If nothing else, I'm doing that."

"Well you *are* a boss lady," my mother agreed. "At least I know you can stand on your own two feet. But shoot, it doesn't hurt to have somebody carry you every once in a while."

It would happen in due time, I encouraged myself. I wasn't so bitter about my past that I couldn't move on. Some things just take....time.

Little did my mother know, I was taking time for the most important person in my life. Me. Except for a few clients, I'd completely stripped my calendar of all unnecessary obligations and appointments. I planned on letting the days play out as they may. If my mother was privy to my plan she'd beg for me to spend the month in Denver. I couldn't do it. Trips to Denver meant endless shopping excursions, late night movies, and begging me to have a baking marathon since I'd inherited my love for all things sweet from her. They were all great things, and when the holidays rolled around I'd give her exactly what she wanted. But right now it was all about Vaughn Holiday. I'd been running on fumes for at least two months, until I decided it was the perfect time to slow things down, live in the moment, and for once forget about trying to take over the world.

The buzz of my oven timer and my front door sounded at the same time. Three knocks on the front door followed. That meant it was Bellamy, my sister from another mother. Where race may have kept us apart, our faith and love of fine cuisine and quirky eating places brought us together.

"Hold on, Bell," I yelled out. Timing was everything and I didn't like my red velvet cupcakes to stay in the oven a minute past their time. I pulled on my oven mitts then slid twenty-four perfectly red, soft and fluffy cupcakes from the oven and set them on wire cooling racks.

"It smells delish in here," Bellamy said as soon as I swung open the door. So you know the entire hallway smells like a bakery. I followed my nose straight to your door."

"I decided to send cupcakes to some of my current and future clients," I told her.

Bellamy pouted. "So that means I can't stuff my face?"

"Girl, please. I always plan for extra."

Bellamy dropped her satchel on the newly reupholstered and refurbished bench that I'd placed at my entryway. She doubled back and took a second look.

"Don't tell me that's the old thing you found at the flea market you drug me to."

"Okay, I won't tell you," I said. I had to admit, it looked amazing.

She stroked the side of one of the deep mahogany wood legs. "I'm impressed. Now if you can find a way that I can creatively house my mountains of books, then I'll officially dub you the DIY queen."

"I'm been scouting for the perfect pieces. I have to go with what speaks to me," I said.

"I can't wait." Bellamy trailed behind me into the kitchen. "I thought you were supposed to be resting," she said when she saw the stacked and labeled boxes of cranpistachio cookies, sugar cookies, peppermint Oreo cookie balls, and chocolate caramel cookies."

"I am resting," said Vaughn. "Baking relaxes me. Today is my day to bake, so that's what I'm doing. Who knows what tonight will hold. "Gingersnaps, sugar cookies."

"Stop," Bellamy said. "Every time you name a dessert, I gain ten pounds, and I have a wedding dress to fit into." That didn't stop her from snagging a sugar cookie from the glass jar instead of a golden apple from the basket beside it.

"I guess you really are taking a break," Bellamy said, sitting down at the sparkling clean bistro table in the corner that was usually the catchall for my contracts, notepads, and laptop. Although I'd set up a corner of my guest room as my at-home office, I preferred to work in the natural light that flooded my kitchen.

Bellamy reached up to twist her once long strawberry blonde tresses into a knot on her head, then looked like she remembered that she'd chopped it off into the cutest page boy cut a week ago.

"I'm exhausted," Bellamy said. "But Esteban bought tickets for one of those mystery dinner theaters so I have to pull myself together. If it were up to me, I'd sip champagne and eat cookies all night."

"You need to go out. You can't work your life away."

"You sound like your mother."

"I do," I admitted. "That seems to be happening more and more."

"It happens to the best of us," Bellamy said. "Every time I speak, I swear I hear Judith Ann Hough."

Bellamy stifled a yawn. I didn't want to point out the extra bags she'd acquired under her eyes, because at this point I knew she was grateful for her job. After almost seven months of unemployment, Bellamy was finally hired as a systems engineer for a major IT consultant company. Her position kept her on an electronic leash;

especially since the telephone company they were contracted with was about to roll out a new program. They called her, texted her, and emailed her. Bellamy was trapped in the web and they wouldn't let her out.

"I'm not going to take on these extra hours for long," she insisted. "I promised myself and I promised my Latino lover." She let the words about her fiancé trill off her tongue with a fake accent. "Of course me and Esteban have been building our savings stockpile, but we still have this wedding to pay for. And the honeymoon. Fiji is calling our names and we're going to enjoy everything that the island has to offer and to the fullest. It's going to take money. Lots of it."

"As your personal real estate agent, I must remind you that one of the most important investments you'll ever make is your home."

"Of course," Bellamy said. "I've learned from the real estate agent extraordinaire. As soon as we hit the three months of marriage mark, we're going to start house-hunting. Planning a wedding and finding a house is too stressful right now."

"I don't blame you." I inhaled deeply, then blew out a cleansing breath. "Woooooossaaaa! Let it go."

I fell back onto the couch and pulled out a pair of footies from the basket at end of my ottoman. For as long as I could remember, my mother had bought me ridiculous-looking footies and socks for every occasion and holiday —birthdays, Valentine's Day, St. Patrick's

Day, Fourth of July, Groundhog Day, Christmas, you name it. She'd even sent me a pair of socks covered in dollar bills once to commemorate April's tax filing deadline. This time I pulled out a pair with bunny ears, an Easter gift, of course. It was a silly tradition but I had to admit I looked forward to what she'd find next. I wiggled my toes as Bellamy came over to join me.

"I bet people would never guess the woman on the front of that magazine wears socks with whiskers and pink puff ball noses," she said, referring to the first quarter issue of the Atlanta Realtors Magazine. "I pray it helps you snag one of the city's top bachelors." Bellamy flipped through the pages even though she'd read the article featuring the *Top 40 Under 40* more than I had.

"Now *you* are sounding like my mother. My knight in shining armor will come when God says its time."

"I won't comment on that." Bellamy ran her fingers through her bangs. "Trace," she said through a faked cough.

"Girlfriend code. You aren't allowed to talk about my past relationship with Trace."

"Why? Because he still makes you feel all warm and fuzzy inside? Tell the truth. In fact, you couldn't lie if you wanted to. I've known you long enough to know that there's still a special place in your heart for him."

"Please," I said, picking up a stack of my business cards. "I can feel all warm and fuzzy with a chocolate fudge brownie."

"Trace *is* a chocolate fudge brownie," Bellamy said.

I almost agreed out loud with her, but that would only fuel her fire. Besides, it was probably going to be a matter of time before Trace messed up like Roderick had. And when Trace did, I didn't want to be part of the fall out. Been there, done that too many times before.

My cell phone rang and vibrated across the coffee table. A picture of Trace appeared on the screen—a selfie that he'd taken of himself. The night I'd denied him the right to change my last name.

"You talked him up," I said, deciding to ignore Trace's call.

"No. That's God sending you a sign," Bellamy said. "You don't want to admit it, but destiny will catch up with you. Aren't you the one that always tells me there's no such thing as a coincidence?"

"There's always an exception," I said. "Trace and I are just friends."

"No, *he* is *your* friend. But to him, you're so much more."

Trace's smiling face lit up my cell phone again.

"You really aren't going to answer that, are you?" Bellamy asked.

"It's not mandatory that you answer the phone because somebody calls," I said, folding my legs under me. I needed to change the subject before Bellamy pulled me into a relationship counseling session.

"So how are you doing with those self-paced Spanish

lessons? Is it working?" "Absolutely," Bellamy said. When my cell phone rang again, Bellamy was still telling me about the times when her fiancé refused to speak English to her because he knew that immersion was the best way for her to learn his native tongue.

Bellamy frowned. "You might want to answer. It could be an emergency."

She was probably right. Trace wouldn't call me so many times if it wasn't important.

"Hello?"

"Hey, Vaughn."

I didn't want to think about Trace being a chocolate brownie and I would never admit that hearing his voice did make me feel warm and fuzzy on the inside because friends aren't supposed to make you feel that way.

Chapter 2

"I was starting to think you didn't want to answer the phone," Trace said.

"I didn't," I admitted, putting him on speaker phone.

He hesitated. "Do you have company?"

"Yes," I said.

I don't think Trace had expected that response. There was a moment of awkward silence. He didn't need to know that it was only Bellamy. I could count the number of men on one hand who'd crossed my threshold in the last six months. Ansel, the maintenance guy, Kiysha's brother, Kenyon, and last week my neighbor Donnie had camped out at my place for about twenty minutes after he accidentally locked himself out. And of course, Trace.

"I'm downstairs in the parking lot. I have a gift I wanted to bring up to you, but I can leave it downstairs at the front desk."

"What is it?" I asked.

"It's a surprise. And you need to open it today."

"Bring it up."

Silence. "Are you sure?"

"Bellamy won't mind."

If I listened closely, I probably would've heard a sigh of relief. I'd never played games with Trace's heart, which is why I was straight-forward when it came to our friendship. I suggested we see other people and he agreed, but to my knowledge he hadn't been out with anyone. I definitely hadn't.

I could hear Trace getting out of his car and closing the door.

"What's the special occasion?" I asked him.

"Nothing really. Let's say it's for your birthday."

"Over a month early?"

"Since you're taking some time off from work, I thought you might want to get out and have some fun. Get dressed up. In real clothes that don't require socks with wiggly eyes."

"To love me is to love my socks," I said. "But no can do. Tonight, I'm going to eat my leftover eggplant parmesan and catch up on some trashy reality TV with no guilt whatsoever until I fall asleep. And yes, I will do it wearing my bunny socks."

"You deserve better on a Friday night," Trace said. "I wish you'd let me be the one to make your nights better. And your days, too."

Bellamy silently clapped her hands together like she was in Trace's corner.

"Trace, don't go there. You're crossing the friends' line. You're making it hard for us to stay friends."

"That's not what I want. That's what *you* want." Had he and Bellamy been having conversations?

Bellamy stood up and mouthed the words, *"I told you."*

"Don't you say that you'll do whatever it takes to make me happy? Us being friends makes me happy."

"Does it?"

I purposefully ignored his question. "See you in a minute."

⌒⟊⟊⟊⟆

"I'm confused," Bellamy said to Trace. "We all know you're madly in love with this woman, but you're willing to send her to an event where she can have her pick from a room full of men. There's something wrong with this picture."

Bellamy handed me back the two tickets to the Matchmakers Mix & Mingle event. I must admit that I was intrigued—but leery—about the opportunity.

"What's the catch?" I asked him.

"There's no catch," Trace said. "I got the tickets as part of a fundraiser." He leaned against the bar stool and folded his arms across his chest. It was easy to see the strong cut of his biceps in his casual Friday work attire. I tried to keep from looking.

"You've made it very clear about where we stand. A few minutes ago you reminded me. Again. So this is my gift to a friend."

He turned away from me, seeming to hide his eyes. His eyes always told the real story. Trace had already eaten two of the three red velvet cupcakes that I'd piped icing on top of. Red velvet was his favorite. He'd devoured each of them in three easy bites and although I knew he could easily eat more, he resisted the urge to take another.

"I don't have anything to wear," I said, snapping open one of my unassembled boxes and applying a label for Vaughn's Delights across the front.

"I've seen your closet. You have plenty. With the tags still on them." Trace tossed his empty cupcake liners in the trash, and seeing the bag full to the top, tied it up and pulled it out of the bin.

"It might be worth going to. Look at it as a networking opportunity," Bellamy chimed in from where she'd been curled up in the corner of the couch. She'd slipped off her shoes and her eyes were glazed over like she was battling sleep.

"That's true. But technically, I'm supposed to be taking a break from work."

Bellamy stood up and shook off her tiredness. "Then go and have a good time and forget about networking. So tonight's not about gingersnaps and sugar cookies like you thought. It's about chocolate brownies." She lifted her eyebrows.

Trace watched me while I piped a dome of cream cheese frosting on another cupcake. I offered it to Bellamy.

"No thanks. I'm done for the night. Besides, I need to save room for dinner."

I perused the details on one of the Matchmakers Mix & Mingle tickets. "This doesn't look good for a single woman. It makes me look desperate, and if there's one thing that I'm not, it's desperate."

"Trust me. The men will know you're not desperate."

"Not like you are for these cupcakes?" I teased, handing him another. He winked at me. My stomach fluttered. If I hadn't seen the lip locking in the parking lot earlier I wouldn't be feeling this way. Right?

"From what I heard, you'll get set up on twelve dates. That's all. Who knows? You might make a love connection."

So now he was concerned about a love life that didn't include him?

"Or, at the very least, eat twelve great meals," Bellamy added. She twisted the top off a cold bottle of water. "There are some places around town I've been meaning to try. Maybe you can write some reviews for me. I'm already a month behind and I don't want to lose any advertisers before I decide to shut the blog down myself."

Bellamy's anonymous foodie blog had started as a hobby while she was unemployed, but now she only kept it up when she could. About every two weeks. She used it to either cheer or jeer local restaurants and eateries. It only took one feature in the Atlanta paper and a tweet by a famous master chef to skyrocket the unique visits to her blog up to about ten thousand per day.

Trace nudged me. "Go ahead. What do you have to lose?"

"My pride. My dignity," I paused a beat, then smiled at Trace. "My celibacy."

"Not funny."

All of a sudden he'd gotten serious. I noticed the tightness in his jawline.

"You're right. If I kept it locked tight for a year with you, you know I wouldn't open up the treasure for a one night stand."

The tension in Trace's face relaxed. Within our year of dating, both my and Trace's vow to stay celibate had been tested and we'd flunked. Twice. Not many times by most people's standards, but two too many based on our relationship with God. Yes, we were two intelligent, focused and determined individuals who loved God first, but apparently we were also in our prime mating years. Warm, strong thighs in a bed felt a lot better than five-hundred thread count sheets. But I knew what was right, and for me, waiting until marriage was best.

Holding Trace's hand, melting into his arms, accepting his warm kisses proved to be too much of a temptation.

Pipe these cupcakes, Vaughn, I told myself, keeping myself from watching his lips.

Even though I'd turned away, now I could feel Trace watching my every move as I started to clean the kitchen.

"I'd love to stay here and chat with you two lovely people but Esteban will be here in an hour, so I'm not the only one who has to get beautiful," Bellamy said. "Vaughn, I suggest you do the same." She swung her head around in a dramatic fashion but her short locks barely moved. She tapped her chin. "I need to find another way to make a dramatic exit," she mused.

"Wait a minute," I said, waving the two tickets in the air. "Who's going with me?"

"Don't look at me," Bellamy said. "I'm spoken for. There's no way I'm stepping up in a room full of muchachos. Esteban wouldn't be a happy man."

Trace said something to Bellamy in Spanish, speaking slowly so she could pick up every word. She responded and they shared a laugh. I, of course, had no idea what they had said.

Trace was fluent in Spanish and conversational German, and although he rarely had the chance to throw around a "Guten Tag" or "Auf Wiedersehen," he got a kick out of the times he and Bellamy could toss around words.

I pointed two fingers at my eyes. "All eyes and conversations on me. I'll go, but I need a partner in crime."

"Kiysha," Trace said matter-of-factly.

Kiysha was not only cousin, but my best friend.

"You're right. I know she'll wish she had more time to get ready, but she can get a lot done in a little time. I've witnessed the transformation firsthand. She can go from sweats to stilettos in record time."

"Then there you go," Bellamy said. "Call or text me when you get home so I know you're in safe."

"I will," I promised.

Bellamy waved. "Have fun."

"I'll make the best of it," I said, before closing and locking the door behind her.

I took a closer look at the tickets. There was a huge red, glittery print of puckered lips on one end, and for the first time I noticed the monetary donation. One hundred dollars per ticket.

"Two hundred dollars?" I asked.

"Read the back," Trace said, pushing the last bit of red velvet cupcake into his mouth. "It's for a good cause."

I flipped the ticket over and read about the nonprofit organization that had been established to 'kiss poverty goodbye.' All of the proceeds were going to provide career training for disadvantaged adults and free educational tutoring for children.

I smiled. "Who's the true cause? Me or the nonprofit organization?"

"I'm not stepping into that trap," Trace said. "Go ahead and call your girl. She'll have her pick of brothers, but there'll also be others. Look at Bellamy and Esteban.

Maybe it's time Kiysha thought outside her box. Don't you agree?"

"Personally, I don't have a problem with it either," I said. "As long as the red blood of Jesus can wash away his sins I could care less about the color of his skin." I took a runway walk down the hallway leading to my bedroom and sauntered back again. I knew Trace was watching every sway of my hips. "As long as the *other* men don't mind lips, hips, and that I'm chocolate-dipped, things will be fine."

"I'm a man who doesn't mind," Trace reminded me. He looked at me for a moment like he regretted giving me the tickets.

Too late. I'd been convinced. "I guess I better call Kiysha and start getting ready."

Surprisingly, Trace nestled up on the long end couch where he could comfortably stretch out his legs. He was settled in like he planned to wait up late into the night for my return.

"What's this all about?" I asked, slapping his knee. "Should I offer you a pillow and blanket?"

"It's been a long day," Trace said, turning up the cuffs on his shirt sleeves. "Actually a long week. They've gotten their money's worth and then some out of this black man this week."

"Because you're good at what you do. The problem comes when they don't depend on you. That's when you should be worried."

"Richard Moseley taught me well," Trace said, dropping his voice an octave to sound like his Dad's deep baritone voice. "If you're going to work, work hard. Don't be the man that's easily replaced. Don't be the last one to arrive in the morning, or the first one leave in the evening."

"He's a smart man," I said.

I'd had the pleasure of spending time with Trace's dad twice during his parents' trips to Atlanta. The man was a wellspring of knowledge and most of the time he spoke like a walking dictionary. Even though Trace had the same chestnut brown skin as his mother, he was the spitting image of his father, down to his hair or lack thereof. The male receding gene had taken its toll on Trace at an early age, but instead of trying to save his hairline he kept his hair cut close, almost bald. It looked good on him, and Trace was mindful about keeping his weekly standing Thursday appointment with his longtime barber, Reggie. I loved that head of his. I used to thump it when he irritated me, or rubbed my hands along the sides when I was in a romantic mood. He'd loved that.

I snapped out of my trance and noticed Trace staring at me again. Studying me.

"Why are you looking at me like that?" he asked.

"Like what?" I said, averting my gaze. "I was looking in your direction. I wasn't really looking at you."

"Okay, if you say so," Trace said, with a hint of a smile on his face.

I was relieved he couldn't read my thoughts, although sometimes I thought he could read what was in my heart even when my words were saying something different. Some things were too good to be true, and I was scared that Trace was one of those things.

"I don't have time to entertain you," I said. "I need to go perform some magic and pull an outfit out of a hat."

"I think you'll be alright," Trace said, reminding me that he'd seen the state of my closet. I wasn't the shopaholic type, but after outing with Kiysha I always returned home with a promise to upgrade my sense of style. Not that I didn't have any. When I wasn't working, I happened to prefer jeans and whatever shirt was comfortable. Cute, but comfortable.

"It's always different when you have to throw together something at the last minute. I've been forced to work with what I've got."

"Trust me," Trace said, "You've got some good things to work with."

"Don't start with me," I said, looking away. Both he and I knew he wasn't talking about clothes.

"Right. Friends."

"Friends," I repeated.

"I've heard friends make the best lovers," Trace said. "My parents were great friends for three years before they crossed that line. Now thirty-five years later they're still best friends." He stood, shook the static cling from the bottom of his pants leg and walked towards me. My heart pattered and I closed my eyes and swallowed easily as he brushed past me.

I'm going to take your car to Bobby's while you get ready."

"You don't have to do that," I said. "It's fine." Bobby was the owner of the neighborhood car detailing salon. Every car rolled out of his lot with an impeccable shine inside and out. It was also the place where I'd met Trace.

"I want to," Trace said.

I'd been meaning to take my car to get detailed for the last three days, but my always-accurate meteorologist predicted scattered showers on the first day, on the second day the wait was too long, and today I'd been in a baking binge.

"Thanks," I said. "You should probably get the spare key from the kitchen drawer so you can let yourself back in."

"I'm on it," Trace said.

I disappeared into my master bath and locked the door while I showered, a habit I'd always had since I'd lived alone. I took my time enjoying the shower, layering my perfumed lotions and scents, and dressing in a pair of black slacks and a silky long-sleeved champagne colored blouse. It was thin enough to wear as a blazer and I was glad that I'd let Kiysha talk me into buying it. No buyer's remorse. It looked as amazing in my bedroom mirror as it had in the department store, not to mention it was perfect for the fall crisp air that had begun to take over the evenings. I slid on two thin, gold bangles, some delicate dangly earring, and walked into the living room for my great reveal.

Trace let out a long, high whistle when he noticed me. There were two glasses of wine waiting on the coffee table and I graciously accepted the glass he handed to me. I swirled it under my nose and inhaled the sweet scent of the pomegranate wine that had become my favorite. The bottle said it was Kosher for Passover. That had to mean something. I justified my once-a-week glass of wine when I stumbled upon a scripture in I Timothy 5:23 about wine being good for the stomach and illnesses. As far as I was concerned, I was drinking to good health.

Trace held up his wine and we clinked glasses.

"To friendship," he said.

"And a great time tonight," I added.

"That, too."

I set my wine glass on a coaster, stretched out my arms, and gave Trace a slow twirl like I was ballerina perched inside of the jewelry box I used to have as a child. In my mommy's true fashion, she'd filled it with some of her customized jewelry and during our dress up play times, I lined bracelets from my wrists to my elbows and cubic zirconia on almost every finger. So gaudy. But gaudy was nowhere in the picture this evening.

"I'm not sure I want you to use those tickets

anymore. All of a sudden this is a bad idea," Trace said, eyeing me from head to toe for the second time.

"That must mean I look nice."

"You look gorgeous. Now give me those tickets back."

"Thank you and no. I'm not giving back my birthday gift." I picked up my glass again and was surprised when Trace lifted his in the air again. "Another toast?"

"To finding love," he added.

"And you seriously want me to find love with someone else?"

"I never said that." Trace tucked in the back of his shirt tail.

We clinked glasses and sipped at the same time. For a quick moment it felt like old times. I broke the gaze between us, then handed him my diamond cross pendant and turned around so that he could fasten it around my neck.

"You smell as good as you look," Trace said, taking his time with the hook.

"Thank you." I wondered if he realized it was the perfume he'd bought for me. I knew most of the women would probably be teetering around in high heels, I'd opted for a simple but fashionable pair of leopard print flats. My walk on the wild side. It was bound to be a long night and I didn't want to lengthen it with aching arches.

Trace hugged me from the side, then kissed my forehead.

"Have fun. Is Kiysha coming with you?"

"You know she jumped at the chance. It didn't take much convincing." I noted the time.

"I better get going, too, so I can have top picks," I joked. "Besides I have to swing by and pick her up."

Trace turned off all the lights in my place except the pendant lights hanging over my bar stools. We rode the elevator in silence down to the lobby where the building security was stationed until midnight. I could see through the secured doors that the darkness had already blanketed the sky. I'd never liked the short days that accompanied the fall and winter seasons. The only things good about chilly and frigid temperatures were homemade chili, comfy sweaters, and cute boots. And of course, warm, homemade cookies and cupcakes.

"Hi, Nathan," I said, noticing that our security guy had shaved his face completely clean. Without facial hair, it knocked at least ten years off his age. Baby face. Dimples. And in love with Kiysha who'd never given him a second look.

"You're coming down empty handed," Nathan said. "I'm confused. And hungry."

"I don't even need to ask who the little birdie was that spilled the beans."

"Bellamy's looking out for me." Nathan patted his mid-section. "Everybody can't be lean and fit like you, man," he said to Trace.

"I have nothing to say," Trace said. "Right now, I

have a stomach full of red velvet."

Nathan's eyes grew wide. Red velvet was his favorite, too.

"I'll bring some down tomorrow," I promised.

Trace opened the door for me, but I stepped aside and let my neighbor and fitness buff, Helene, whisk into the building. As usual she was wearing skin tight exercise leggings, a t-shirt, and some kind of calorie burning watch. Last Christmas, she'd given me the cutest pedometer watch to track the 10,000 steps a day that I was supposed to be taking, but after three months, it had found its way to the top drawer of the side table in my bedroom.

"Don't you guys look nice," Helene gushed. "I've always thought you guys were the cutest couple." She wagged a finger at Trace. "She's a keeper."

"I tried," Trace said, pretending to be defeated.

"If at first you don't succeed, try and try again," Helene said.

"Advice taken," Trace said.

"Helene," I said in a voice of playful warning.

"I'll keep my nose out of your love life when you decide to try my spin class again."

"That's blackmail, Helene. The last time I swear I saw my life flash before my eyes."

"I'm sure you did," Helene agreed. "You're out of shape. But if you think you've got a cute little body now, wait until I flatten that tummy, rip those thighs, and tighten that booty." She put a solid two-hand grip on her own backside and turned it around for us to admire. I had to admit, they were definitely buns of steel.

"What other kind of blackmail do you know that can give you results like that?"

"Soon," I said.

"I'm holding you to your word, Vaughn," Helene said before speed-walking to the elevator.

"It's almost time for the moment of truth," I said. "Let me go and see what this Mix and Mingle event is all about."

I clicked my remote and my alarm chirped off. My car gleamed even brighter with the help of the street light above my designated parking spot. It looked as spotless as it had a little over a year ago when I'd driven the midnight blue machine off the car lot. After bumming around in a Toyota hand-me-down during college and the post years afterwards, I'd promised myself I'd treat myself to a luxury vehicle when I had the money to do so. Seven years and two vehicles later, my Mercedes Benz was worth every penny.

"I owe you one," I said, playfully bumping my hips against Trace's.

"I'll add it to your tab," Trace said. He opened my door for me and waited until I was situated and buckled before he closed it. I let my tinted windows slide down slowly, and then started the engine. It purred so quietly that if it hadn't been for the dashboard lights it would have been hard to tell that the car was on.

"Wish me luck," I said, shifting the car in reverse. Trace kissed two fingers and held up a peace sign. I returned his gesture my blowing him a kiss. He pretended to swoon and fall against his car. That's where I left him.

I activated the hands-free device to call Kiysha.

"We are two Atlanta women who are single and ready to mingle. I'm on my way, girlie," I said. "Let's see if we can find a match made in heaven."

Chapter 3

"I should've stayed at home with my fuzzy slippers," I said after one glance around the dimly lit room. Even with the sparse lighting, I could sense the meat market atmosphere. I took two steps backward.

"Oh no," Kiysha whispered and grabbed my arm. "You aren't about to abandon me now and you're the one who invited me. Besides, you had no business giving me your car keys and I'm not giving them up."

Kiysha loved oversized purses, which was the reason I'd given her the keys since my envelope-sized clutch could barely hold more than my ID, a tube of lipstick, and a travel size pack of tissue. If I'd kept my keys, I would be able to stage a standoff inside of the car, instead of inside of here. The men swarmed around like they were bees and the women were honey.

"I promise I'll still be outside whenever you're ready to go. I have the radio to keep me company and I'm sure there's a novel tucked somewhere in the back seat pocket. I'll be fine."

"You'll do no such thing. If I have to stick it out, then you have to stick it out, Vaughn. You back out of everything that makes you uncomfortable and turn your nose up at people who aren't exactly like you. You can be a little bougie sometimes."

Kiysha was probably right. A teeny bit.

Two men in freshly dry-cleaned slacks, button downs and casual blazers walked by. "And there are two reasons why we should stay. Mix. Mingle. You said it yourself on the way here. You might not find a love connection—which you don't need anyway since you have a man who adores you—but you might find a new client."

I should be mixing flour and measuring sugar, I thought. "I don't think marble floors, tray ceilings, and finished basements are on the minds of the men in here."

"You never know," Kiysha said. She parked her hands on her hips. "Settle down and enjoy your birthday."

"My birthday isn't for another month and a half."

"Tell that to Trace. This is his gift to you, not mine. But if you don't intend to celebrate, then I'll do it for you. I'm not going to waste an outfit like this."

Kiysha was decked out head to toe in an off-white ensemble.

"I do look fabulous, don't I? Go ahead and admit it,"

Kiysha purred. "Now wouldn't it be so selfish of you to deny all of these men my presence? There are so many of them and only one of me. How ever will I choose?" She pressed her hand against her heart like a Southern Belle.

Eye candy passed us at that exact moment. A surge of attendees entered the room at the same time and I took in the finest of the fine and those that most women would consider average. I'd never been the superficial type. A man didn't have to have the looks to grace the cover of GQ magazine for me to give him a chance. I'd learned long ago that brains could take you farther than brawn.

And then there were the men who….the men who left me speechless.

"This should be an interesting night," I said watching a man with a bright red jacket and sequined black bowtie strut by.

"That could be an understatement," Kiysha said. She gave him a pained smile when he turned around to check her out. "Keep walking, grandpa," she said under her breath.

I laughed and hooked my arm through hers. "You might be counting out a good man."

"I'll count out any man who looks like he's supposed to be dancing back up behind Gladys Knight."

Kiysha had been my side kick through every dating disaster and relationship drama I'd ever cried myself through. I'd asked her to be my maid of honor and bridal consultant for my "almost" wedding three years ago. Kiysha had been my accomplice when I'd decided to be the runaway bride. And I'd run for good reason. I'd never known that my fiancé had been cheating on me for almost as long as we'd been dating. Me. The one who prided myself on not being gullible and for smelling a rat from a mile away. Even Kiysha hadn't seen any red flags.

If Roderick hadn't approached me in the parking lot when I was leaving the real estate office, I would've floated down the wedding aisle in ignorant bliss and vowed before God to stick with Roderick for better or for worse.

I cried. He apologized. We wept in each other's arms and dried each other's tears. Two months later his tears had dried, but mine hadn't. On our wedding day, I was twenty-three minutes from the organ's first chord when I called it off. Actually Kiysha called it off, helped me change out of my gown, and snuck me out the back door where my mother was waiting in the back seat of the limo to ride with us to the airport.

My Punta Cana, Mexico honeymoon quickly turned to a girlfriend get-away. I cried my last tears about Roderick while I was there and let the attentive Caribbean island men and the endless wave of the ocean wash away all of my regrets.

"Hello, back to Earth, girlfriend," Kiysha said. "You checked out on me there for a minute. And while you were checked out, the cutest little chocolate drop was checking *you* out."

I unzipped my jacket, then straightened the front of my blouse. "There's one benefit to this whole thing that I didn't think about."

"What's that?" Kiysha asked.

"I haven't posted anything to my blog for over two months. This could be the rebirth of my musings on love and relationships. I have a feeling some things are about to change."

I'd launched my blog at the same time Bellamy started her foodie blog. It was more cathartic than anything and easy for me to vent since I could hide behind the anonymity of the World Wide Web. After all, I was one of Atlanta's up and coming top real estate agents. I wasn't supposed to have relationship issues.

"As your closest family member and girlfriend I should be straight up with you." Kiysha and I spotted an empty table at the same time and headed in that direction. "Nobody reads your blog but me, your mama, and your three country cousins in Alabama who want to live vicariously through you."

"Blogging is the way of the world these days. Plenty of people have built a name for themselves with their social media prowess."

"Then do your thing," Kiysha said. "And I suggest we place a friendly bet?"

"Which is?"

"If you don't meet and go on a date with at least ten men, then you have to give me the dollhouse?"

"The dollhouse?" No, she didn't.

Kiysha had been trying to get her hands on *my* dollhouse for at least ten years. Our paternal grandfather was a master carpenter, and had built the dollhouse with his own hands. Although it wasn't an exact replica, it resembled the house of our grandparents. Over the years he'd added custom built furniture and my grandmother had used scrap pieces of fabrics to sew curtains, linen for the beds, and clothes for our dolls. When he'd passed away, I'd been the first cousin to arrive at their home. In my quest to find something to cherish as a memory, I'd claimed the dollhouse. It was mine.

"You've lost your mind," I told Kiysha. "The dollhouse is mine."

"You're scared. You know you'll punk out and not finish the dates."

"I won't," I said, determined to prove her wrong. "You've got a bet."

Kiysha popped her lips. "I can't wait to get my dollhouse back."

My cousin wasn't about to get off that easy. "And if I complete my ten dates, then you should plan on handing over that Louis Vuitton purse. You know the one."

Kiysha clutched the top of her blouse like she was appalled. "Oh, you want to play dirty."

"So you're worried?"

Kiysha playfully rolled her eyes at me. "Bet. So let's get this bet moving and find some boys for this blog."

"Men. We're looking for men," I corrected her.

Kiysha sucked in her waist so that her bust line lifted five inches higher. "Another correction. The men will be looking for us." She subtly turned her back to a man who was trying to get her attention. "But not that one."

If a suitor wasn't at least six-feet-two, Kiysha would never give him the time of day. She was five-nine and the poor dude may have been five-feet-six. I couldn't knock a little man with a big ego for trying.

"Please tell me he's walking away," Kiysha said.

"He's already gone," I assured her.

"At least he can take a hint."

"You shouldn't be so superficial," I told Kiysha. "There's more to people than their physical appearance."

"Yada, yada," Kiysha said. "That sounds good, but there has to be some kind of physical attraction in a mate. Let's keep it real."

"Being short is something he can't control, but he can control his heart, how he lives his life, and how he treats his woman."

Kiysha stuffed her hand in her purse and pulled out a mint. She slid the paper off and slipped it into her mouth. "Then let me call him over for *you*." She stood.

"You wouldn't dare," I said.

"Oh, you know I would."

She would. "Behave. We're celebrating my birthday, remember?"

I doubt Kiysha heard me. It seemed she'd caught the

eye of another admirer from across the room. And he was tall. Skyscraper tall.

"Why is it that you always seem to pull the most handsome person in a room?"

"Because I'm usually the prettiest in the room," Kiysha teased. "But I'm still single so obviously beauty will only take you so far." Kiysha inhaled deeply again, flattening her stomach and lifting her ample bosom even higher than the push-up bra had done. "No need for jealousy. You'll have a set of these one day when you grow up."

I shook my head. "I'm almost thirty-six. Unless I make a major purchase, I'm pretty sure I've got the set I'm going to have for the rest of my life."

Kiysha waved my comment away with the flick of her hand. "Who knows what will happen after you have kids. I've seen women's bodies make some drastic turns after having a baby, which you know is something I'll never do."

Kiysha was adamant about letting anyone she'd been in a serious relationship know that she had no desire to have children. In my opinion her reasons were way to shallow, but she was entitled to live her life through her own convictions. In her own words—she didn't want to mess up her figure and she wanted to be free to travel at the drop of a dime. She never wanted to choose onesies over handbags. She enjoyed late nights and sleeping in on late mornings. She would be an auntie and a godmommy but that was it.

"Where are your contact cards?" Kiysha asked about the business sized cards they'd given us at the front door.

"Right here." I patted my clutch. I pulled out my stack of twelve cards and a ballpoint pen. The male greeters at the registration desk had instructed us to write our names and our best form of contact on each card. I wrote my first name only and an email address that I used for junk email like receiving offers and coupons from stores and restaurants.

"I'm not using mine," Kiysha decided. I followed her eyes. I knew why.

"I don't think it's fair to waste the time of the other men here. I'm going to be busy. She pointed to the skyscraper. "Over in that area. Waiting to be found," she said before slinking away.

No matter how many times Kiysha was sucker punched by love, she was always willing to take another chance.

I looked around for a way to comfortably ease myself into a conversation with someone. Thankfully, a nearby gentleman came to my quick rescue.

"So it looks like you've been abandoned. Don't feel bad. I was kicked to the curb, too."

He stopped a passing hostess who was carrying miniature chilled cans of soda on a tray. He took off two ginger ales and handed one to me along with a short straw. "Bryant Sims," he said.

"Nice to meet you, Bryant. I'm Vaughn."

"No last name?" he inquired.

"Of course," I said.

Bryant waited until he realized I had no intention of giving it to him. He chuckled. "I can't say I blame you for withholding that piece of information. It's a crazy world, with some even crazier people."

"True," I agreed. I crossed my legs and second guessed my decision to wear flats.

"So I saw you when you walked in, Vaughn. You caught my eye immediately."

"Is that so?" I asked. "Why is that?"

"For one you're a gorgeous woman naturally because I can actually see your face and not all that makeup. And secondly, I noticed the shoes. I couldn't help it. Back in the day, they were my mama's favorite."

I rotated my ankle. "Thank you. Your mother had good taste."

"Does wearing animal print mean you have a wild side?" Bryant asked.

"I wouldn't necessarily say that," I said, popping the tab to my ginger ale and inserting the straw. The first sip tickled my nostrils. "It means this is the most comfortable pair in my closet."

"Good choice." He nodded his head. "Look at the woman over there with the red dress. She should've thought about the same thing."

Poor thing, I thought, watching her teeter by like her

stilettos were three sizes too small. I'd give her another thirty minutes before she called it quits.

"So what do you think about the change in the rules?" Bryant asked after we'd sat quietly for a moment surveying our surroundings.

"What change?" I asked. "I though it was simple. Mix and mingle with at least twelve people and possibly set up twelve different dates."

"You must've missed the announcement," Bryant said.

"Enlighten me."

"You see those boxes up front?"

I followed his gaze to rows of at least one hundred gift-wrapped boxes lined at the front of the room. Each box had a number on the front.

"Each of the men has been assigned a number, but the women don't know which number. You're supposed to put your contact cards in twelve random gift boxes

"Are you serious? So basically we'll have twelve blind dates."

Bryant nodded. "Exactly."

That was a bad idea. Whoever had come up with it needed to be fired from the committee.

"So what's the point of mixing and mingling here?" I asked.

"Forty-four."

"Excuse me?" I asked, confused.

"Forty-four. That's my box number. Now at least

one of your dates won't be blind," Bryant said.

"Is that cheating?"

"You think we're the only ones cheating? Every man will do it. At least once."

"Cheat, you mean?"

"In life, maybe. But in here, for sure," Bryant corrected quickly. "I know tonight is for charity, but we've put out a hundred bucks. The least we can do is find a connection with one woman. And that one woman can skip the boxes altogether and give a man her phone number directly." He opened his blazer and revealed a pocket. "A contact card would fit perfectly right here."

I gave him a school-girl smile before I pulled a single card out of my purse, drew a star in the corner of it, and handed it to him.

"Still no last name *and* no phone number." Bryant noted.

"And no exceptions," I said. "Despite your pick-up game, you're still a stranger. Even though I have to admit there's something familiar about you. I bet we have a lot in common. That still doesn't mean you're getting my number, though. Not yet."

"We're definitely kindred spirits." When Bryant smiled his thick eyebrows met in the middle.

Bryant and I ended up having small talk for about another thirty minutes before we went our separate ways. Most of the men were running around like kids in a candy store, so I found a table in the corner and did my best to act interested in whatever man was courageous enough to approach my table. My mind was buzzing with blog post topics and I knew where I'd start first. So many women were still single in Atlanta because the men had too many choices.

I was tempted to leave the Mix and Mingle with my remaining eleven contact cards, but I kept hearing Kiysha's voice in my head. "Live a little." I went up front and dropped my cards in the boxes with the prettiest wrapping paper.

Chapter 4

"You didn't text me when you got home. I was worried about you."

Trace was my first call on Saturday morning, and though I was usually up and starting my day by nine o'clock, it was nine forty-five and I couldn't bring myself to roll out of bed yet. "Evidently you weren't that worried or you would've tried to get in touch with me. What did you do last night?"

He paused. It felt kind of awkward. Trace cleared his throat.

"Hello? Is this thing on?" I asked, tapping the receiver of my phone with my fingernail.

Trace coughed. The truth was stuck in his throat. I don't think Trace could lie if I paid him. Then Trace started his morning round of sneezing. Every morning—for whatever reason—Trace sneezed at least six times in a row. It was the craziest genetic thing I'd ever heard of.

His dad and granddad did the same thing.

"Dare I ask?" I added when he was in mid-sneeze. I slipped down under my sheets but could hear Kiysha rambling around in my kitchen. She was part of the reason I was still in the bed. We'd had one of our old-fashioned nights of laughter and confessions. My mom always used to tell me that having a good girlfriend was good for a woman's soul. She was right. I'd cackled until my throat was sore and my stomach ached.

The man of Kiysha's dreams ended up being the man of many women's dreams. Three women to be exact. Three wives, of whom Kiysha didn't find out about until he'd wooed her all night. He was in some strange religion that encouraged multiple wives and he wanted Kiysha to be his fourth one. I made her put her hand on the Bible to swear she wasn't making it up.

"One of my colleagues has been wanting to introduce me to his sister for a while," Trace said. "She called me last night on her way home from work and we ended up going out to dinner."

A lump caught in my throat. I forced it back down. "So she called you and asked you out? No need to wait for chivalry, I guess," I said.

Trace corrected me. "Actually *I* asked Stephanie to dinner."

That lump tried to force its way into my throat again. I swallowed it again.

Stephanie. That name could go both ways—she

could be either the innocent or sinister type, depending on how you said it. Sssssssstephnanie, I hissed.

"And here I thought I was the only woman who held your heart," I teased.

"You do have my heart, but since you're choosing not to do anything with it, I have to keep my options open."

Why did he have to say that? I watched the ceiling fan blades turn in a dizzying whir.

"So I bet those Mix & Mingle tickets you gave me were really yours?"

"Actually I bought them to support the cause. I thought about going, but by Wednesday I knew I didn't want to be bothered. I didn't feel like being in a crowd. But you know that. When I have the option, I like to hang with a few folks. Or one." A beat passed. "So did you have a good time?"

"Actually it wasn't as bad as I thought it was going to be. I didn't make any business connections, but I did meet a few interesting men."

"Interesting in what way? As in crazy or intriguing?"

"Both," I admitted. "And they had these new so-called rules." I filled Trace in on the new twist with the contact cards and numbered boxes.

"And you did it?"

"I played by the rules, except for once. That's the guy I'm meeting up with at Stone Mountain today."

"He couldn't come up with something more

original?" Trace said.

"What about your date? Dinner and a movie. There was nothing special about that either."

"Only dinner at Chow Baby. No movie," Trace confirmed. "You can't learn much about someone if you spend most of your time sitting in the dark watching a movie. Besides, Stephanie had a rough week, too. We agreed to make it an early night."

Why did he have to say her name again?

I'd been the one to pull the plug on our relationship and push Trace into the friend category, but for some reason I was feeling some kind of way about knowing he'd gone out with another woman. Maybe this wasn't the first time he'd taken someone out since our split, but it was the first time he admitted it. I always wondered how it would feel when I realized he might be moving on. Now I knew. It would take some time to get used to, but I'd have twelve upcoming dates to help me do it. I was rolling my dice that at least half of the men were as spectacular as Bryant.

Speaking of Bryant, I had some cleaning and errands I wanted to do before it was time for our date that evening.

"I can smell bacon and biscuits and who knows what else taking over my kitchen so I'm going to indulge myself," I said. Kiysha's cooking was definitely luring me out of bed.

"No breakfast invitation?" Trace said.

"Not this time," I said. I wanted to add, "Let Stephanie cook you breakfast," but I didn't want to let his first taste for the morning be a spoonful of sarcasm.

"Have fun tonight," Trace said.

I could tell by his voice that he didn't really mean it.

"I will. Talk to you later."

I kicked my sheets to the bottom of the bed, then went into the bathroom to swipe a warm washcloth across my face. Despite my sleepy efforts to clean my face last night, the remains of my black waterproof mascara and a little makeup crud in the corner of my eyes still remained.

I was headed out to stuff my face when Trace called one last time.

"What's your home remedy for a sore throat?" he said. "I can feel a little tingle and I need to stop it before it gets worse." He coughed. Yuck. He sounded contagious.

"The next time you go out on a date with Stephanie you should probably keep your lips to yourself," I told him. "Some things you catch, you can't get rid of."

"I don't kiss and tell," Trace said.

Trace couldn't fool me. He was a gentleman and hadn't even kissed me on the first date, so I seriously doubted that he and Stephanie had locked lips. Then of course, Stephanie could've been the aggressor since she'd been the one to call him last night.

Still, the thought of Trace's lips sent me in a

flashback. Trace was a great kisser. He was slow and careful about it. Never in a rush. He let his lips do all of the talking and they had plenty to say. I'd never been one to mush faces with a lot of men, but I didn't need to, to know that he was one of the best. He didn't kiss me until he'd walked me to my door after our seventh date. Lucky number seven.

"Bye, Trace," I said, before nostalgia could get the best of me.

My nose had correctly sniffed the bacon, but instead of biscuits there were scrambled eggs and sweet potato pancakes. Kiysha was an expert at making pancakes that were just the right thickness and consistency. Fluffy. Mine always ended up too flat and either overdone or too doughy.

"Good Morning sunshine," Kiysha said when I padded down the hallway into the living room. She was turning into Kassandra, her mother. Kassandra called everyone Sunshine or Darling.

"You should sleep over every Friday," I suggested. "I can get used to a Saturday morning breakfast spread." She handed me a paper plate with my food already prepared.

"Don't say a word," Kiysha said, when I frowned at the paper plate. "I cook, you clean. I'm trying to make it easier for you. I don't want you going on your date with rough dishpan hands. What if this Bryant guy is the affectionate, touchy-feely type? You don't want your hands to feel like lizard skin. "

"That's why I have the dishwasher," I said. Unless I was at a cookout where paper goods and Styrofoam were the norm, I'd always preferred eating off of my real stoneware plates. Nice dishes were meant to be enjoyed, and in my opinion food always looked and tasted better on real dishes.

"Eat your food." Kiysha chastised me like a child.

I was too hungry to argue, and Kiysha wouldn't listen anyway. I poured two tall glasses of orange juice.

"I'm kind of nervous about this date tonight with Bryant. I hope he looks as fine today as he did last night. You know how you can see somebody the second time and be disappointed? God, please don't let that happen."

"He was cute. I can vouch for that, so your eyes didn't deceive you. Focus on having a good time. You don't have to worry about teetering around in heels and trying to be over the top at Stone Mountain. You can be you. Dress like you would if you were going out with Trace." Kiysha found a straw to stick in her glass. She drank everything from a straw—sweet tea, soda, orange juice—because she claimed years from now the rest of us would have stained teeth and eroded enamel.

"Why would you bring Trace up? His name isn't going to be in my vocabulary for the rest of the day."

"My bad," Kiysha said. "I can't help that you can't see what I can see."

I ignored Kiysha's comment and bit into my sweet

potato pancakes. I turned my attention toward the TV where Kiysha was watching a DIY show about turning your trash into treasure.

"I hope you guys have a good time," Kiysha said. "I haven't even thought about going to Stone Mountain since we made that resolution last year to climb the mountain every Saturday for a year—except in rain, snow, sleet, or hail."

"We lasted all of two months," I chuckled. "Some grand plan we had. I'd be too tired to make the drive so early on Saturday mornings. Six o'clock was probably too ambitious."

"It wasn't the time. You've never had a problem rising with the sun when you have to get something done. Let's keep it real. You were too tired because on Friday nights you were out late with Trace at the movies, or going to Jazz at the High, or seeing a play at the Fox, or—"

"Okay, I get your point. But I don't have that problem anymore." I squeezed half of my regular serving of syrup on my pancakes. I was still on a sugar high from me and Kiysha's late night sugar binge.

"Being wined and dined around the city was a good problem to have. Plenty of women in Atlanta wish they had that problem. Heck, I wish I had that problem. And with a man who's not trying to make me part of his harem," Kiysha added.

"Moving on," I said. "I need to find something to

wear. Just because this date is outside doesn't mean I want to look like I'm headed out into the wild blue yonder." Kiysha knew the inventory in my closet better than I did. She was a shop-a-holic and though I usually agreed to come along to window shop, I usually left the mall with as many bags as she did.

"Wear a pair of jean capris or shorts with that cute yellow polo type shirt you bought from the Gap last week. And don't wear the shortie shorts. Those things show off half of your behind. You don't want to ruin your Christian girl image. Not on the first date anyway."

"For your information, I only wear my shortie shorts when I'm home," I said, helping myself to the last piece of bacon. "And I think I like the white capris better."

"White? By the end of the day you'll end up looking like you had an accident in your pants. Stone Mountain is dusty. No light colored shorts."

"You're right," I said. "I didn't even think about that."

"So now I'm your personal chef and fashion consultant. I'll send you my invoice."

"Put it on my tab," I said, resisting the urge to squeeze more syrup onto my pancakes. "I think we'll have a nice time. Since you confirmed Bryant is eye candy and I already know he can hold a sustaining, intelligent conversation, that alone shoots him to the top of the list."

"What does he do? Does he have any money?"

"He's an entrepreneur. He owns his own business."

"Oh, so he's broke," Kiysha laughed.

"In case you need reminding, you're looking at an entrepreneur who isn't broke. We're in Atlanta. The home of young, black professionals."

"And the fakers."

"You should expect better of people," I said, even though her words were true. People in Atlanta were known to take "fake it 'til you make it" to another level.

Kiysha swiveled around in her chair and I noticed as usual that she wasn't wearing any socks. I never understood people who could walk around the house in bare feet, since I was a person whose feet were always cold.

"I'm a realist. And I expect that some men—and women—can be really shady. You should keep your ears and your eyes open on all these blind dates."

"You're right," I said. "I'll make sure you know where I'm going at all times. But I didn't see those red flags with Bryant," I said. "We had a lot in common. It's like we're cut from the same cloth."

"I'm not going to rain on your parade," Kiysha said. She squeezed too much dish detergent on the skillet she'd used for the pancakes. "If there's one thing I can say—besides that *one* exception—you know how to choose good men."

"The good men actually choose me," I said, raising my hands to push a stretch through the length of my body.

"Right. You're the one with the commitment issues."

"I wish you'd stop saying that."

"What did I tell you? I'm a realist. I live in the truth, the whole truth, and nothing but the truth."

"And I know that oh so well," I said.

"So since you know me, I'm free to warn you not to bore Bryant to death with your latest analysis of the real estate market, or give him a workshop on how to use rental properties to create residual income for his future grandchildren."

"Too late," I smiled. "But he asked me, and he seemed interested."

"Was that really interest in his eyes or were his eyes glazed over with boredom?"

"If I didn't love you *and* your food so much, I'd kick you out," I teased.

"You'd never do that," Kiysha said. "But this morning you don't have to because I'm on my way out anyway. I have a spa appointment and my favorite massage therapist is coming in especially for me. I'm telling you nobody in the city can knead out these kinks like Titus. He has hands—and buns—of steel. Too bad he's ugly."

"I could use a sea salt body scrub," I said, checking the time. "Now that spring has sprung I'm ready for that glow and I'm pretty sure I have some money left on the gift card Trace bought me for my birthday last year."

"See. Trace's name pops up in your vocabulary even

when you don't want it to," Kiysha said. "And isn't it funny that you're using a gift from one man to get spiffed up to go out with another man."

I dumped my empty plate in the trash. "No, what would really be funny is if there was an actual love connection between me and Bryant. And it would all be Trace's fault."

⚬⚬⚬

I was waxed, buffed and scrubbed to perfection at the spa before I returned home for a nap. By four o'clock, I was rested and waiting for Bryant at the inside entrance of Stone Mountain Park. He arrived about five minutes after me, wearing a pair of basketball shorts and a CAU Alumni t-shirt. His calves looked like he climbed Stone Mountain on a daily basis.

"Long time, no see," he joked, pulling me into a side hug as he walked up.

"It's been what? A whole twenty-one hours?"

"You look nice. Even prettier than I remembered. Sometimes the lighting at those events can play tricks on you."

"Why was I thinking the same thing?" I bent down to tie my shoe but Bryant was quick to stoop and do it for me.

"I'm glad I didn't disappoint. And you didn't disappoint either," I said, as I noted he had a full head of hair in his crown. No thinning as far as I could tell. That was a good thing.

I followed Bryant to the ticket booth and waited while he purchased two passes that would allow us to go to almost every attraction at the park. I assumed he thought we'd have a great time. And we did. Kiysha would be happy to know that I didn't bore him with real estate and he didn't bore me with details about his contractual job at a tech company downtown.

The hours with Bryant passed by quickly, and though I never thought we'd still be at the park when the sun began to set, I readily accepted his invitation to hang around until the Laser Show.

"We can go grab a blanket from the trunk of my car if you'd like," I offered.

"That's cool. I wouldn't want any insects nibbling as those honey brown legs of yours. You don't have a single scratch on them. You must've been one of those prissy girls growing up."

"Not exactly," I said. "My mother was obsessed with cocoa butter and Vitamin E oil. It really works."

Bryant gave a long train whistle when we arrived at my car. "Real estate isn't treating you that bad. Nice ride. And it shines like you just drove it off the lot."

I popped the trunk to reveal not only a blanket, but an organized bin of emergency items: a few bottles of water, dried apricot and cranberry snacks, a novel, a book of crossword puzzles, and of course the regular car items like jumper cables, a roadside hazard light, flashlight and tire jack.

From the time I cartwheeled out of the driver's license bureau, newly armed with my license and the month later when I had my first used car—a Toyota Corolla—my mother had taught me to keep a well-stocked trunk with emergency items. I'd never been so thankful for her advice than the time I was forced to spend ten hours on the highway during the notorious Snowpocalypse that shut down the Atlanta highways. I didn't get much sleep but at least my gas tank was full, I was warm, had food, and something to do to pass the time away.

"I could take some pointers from you," Bryant said. "The only things in my trunk are some jumper cables and some sweaty gym clothes."

"My mom taught me well."

"Do you always listen to your mother?' Bryant asked me, tossing the blanket over his shoulder.

"Not always. But she's right about a lot of things. And the older I get, the more I realize how much we are alike. Scary, but true. Only she's a little more of a firecracker."

I'd barely finished my sentence when Bryant leaned down and pressed his lips against mine. He started to pull away slightly, but I placed my hand on the back of his neck and pulled him in for another. Mouths closed. Sweet. Perfect.

"That was unexpected," I said, suddenly hoping that my breath didn't smell like the onions grilled inside of the chicken quesadillas I'd eaten for lunch.

"Those are the best ones. Thought I better go in for it before I changed my mind."

"I'm glad you didn't change your mind."

We walked nearly shoulder to shoulder back to the open grassy area where the grounds were populated with both couples and families. Bryant grabbed my hand and we mazed through the growing crowd of people and found a spot where we could make an easy exit once the show was over. Bryant spread the blanket across the grass, helped me down, then eased down until he was reclining back on his elbows.

He had the thickest eyebrows. Kiysha loved a man with thick eyebrows. I leaned back beside him so that we could both take selfies with our cell phones. I made sure I got a good clear shot of Bryant so I could text it to Kiysha and Bellamy as soon as I got back to my car.

"So you told me you've been in Atlanta since you were about six, but you never said where you lived before that," I said.

"Believe it or not, I'm originally from Denver, Colorado."

"You're kidding me? I'm from Denver, too. But I guess you don't remember too much of your life there."

"Nothing but the drama. When my parents divorced I ended up leaving and moving to the east coast with my dad. He pretty much kept me away from my mom and her side of the family. I don't think my dad ever felt that he measured up to the standards of the Holidays."

Did he say the Holidays? I gulped. I had a weird feeling in my stomach.

"The Holidays?" I repeated again to make sure I'd heard him correctly.

"They Holidays are my mom's side of the family. I'm a Sims."

The light turned on in my head.

"What's your Mom's name? Please don't tell me it's Bonnie."

"Okay, I won't tell you," Bryant said, sitting upright now. His eyebrows furrowed. "But it is. Is there something I should know?"

"My last name is Holiday," I admitted. "I have a feeling we're related, but Auntie Bonnie's son's name was Corey."

"Oh. Dang." He leaned away from me like he'd been struck with a flashback, too. "That's me. Corey Bryant Sims."

We stared at each other as a flood of memories rushed back into my mind. His thick eyebrows. My mom and all my aunts had them. Corey—also known as Bryant—and I had built towers of Legos on Auntie Bonnie's kitchen floor. We'd gotten in trouble when Corey flooded the inside of his dad's truck when we were pretending to be in a drive-through car wash. I vaguely remember the day my mom told me Corey had moved away with his Dad and she didn't know when I'd get to see him again. That turned out to be never. I put my hand up to my mouth. That soft, tender peck on the lips that had given me the fuzzies—had come from my cousin.

Chapter 5

I showed Bellamy the picture of me and Bryant, aka Corey. "He's a cutie," she said.

"That's no consolation," I whined. "We're related. And I kissed him."

"At least it didn't involve tongue," she said, enlarging the picture of my phone. "Look at it this way. Your first Mix & Mingle date may not have been a love connection, but it was a family reunion. That's nice."

"That's not nice. It's nasty. I can understand trying to look at the positive sides of things, but you're trying a little too hard. The entire thing feels so weird right now. I'm not even sure I could look at him again."

Bellamy was multi-tasking as usual—painting her nails, sending a text message, and answering calls from her work-assigned cell phone. All of this before it was time to leave for church. On Sunday mornings we usually carpooled and also alternated on who would cook breakfast, but we had to drive separate cars today since I had two Mix and Mingle dates following church service. The first thing I planned to do was ask the men about their family history.

"Things can only go up from here," Bellamy said like she was reading my mind.

Maybe Bellamy was right. What could be worse than kissing cousins?

As usual, Sunday morning worship put me in better spirits. God had a plan for everything so I finally decided to look at finding Corey—Bryant—as God's way of beginning to mend his relationship with my family. When the weirdness of the situation wore off, I'd contact him about the Holidays family reunion next summer.

After church, I headed back downtown to Paschal's Restaurant for the first of my Mix & Mingle dates planned for today. Bellamy and I had dined at the historic eatery plenty of times so I didn't feel pressured to use my discriminating palate to write a review for her blog. Their food was down home, Southern cooking. Period.

"Okay, girl, I'm here." Kiysha had insisted I call her before my outings today to make sure I wasn't going to be sucking face with another cousin, as if she had some type of radar via phone. She was relieved that it was a cousin from my mother's side of the family, claiming she'd never get over knowing I'd kissed one of her relatives.

"Do you see what's his name?"

"Stephen," I said. "But I'm here about fifteen minutes early so I doubt he's here yet. He told me he drives a red truck and I don't see one in the parking lot or the valet area.

"Good. Then that means you'll get first look," Kiysha said.

"Despite what he looks like, I'm still going inside. I've learned better than to judge a book by its cover."

"You speak for yourself. When I look at a potential boo, I want to have sweet dreams that night, not nightmares. I don't see why you're trying to act like looks don't matter."

Leave it to Kiysha to make a valid point, but I still wasn't going to ditch out on a date because I might not be physically attracted to the guy. That was rude. "I'm going to stick this Mix and Mingle challenge out until the last date. You never know. Date number twelve could end up being the man of my dreams."

"We already know who the man of your dreams is, or should be. But I'll humor you. Who's the dream guy later today?" Kiysha asked.

"A guy named Carlton. He sent me an email and invited me to a play at his church."

"Oh, he's one of those." Kiysha chuckled to herself.

"What do you mean by that?"

"Super spiritual. What kind of man invites a woman out to church for their first date? He's probably going to make you pin a doily on your head, too."

"Oh shut up," I laughed. "I actually thought it was a nice idea."

"You *would*," Kiysha said.

I flipped down the sun visor and fluffed my hair. The honey brown streaks I'd let my stylist experiment with caught the sunlight. I had to admit it complimented my skin tone perfectly. Yvette would definitely get a heftier tip next time.

I glanced out the window and noticed a red long-bed, double cab Chevy truck. That had to be Stephen. The tint was too dark for me to see inside, but I immediately noticed the shiny red and black front tag boasting that he was a Big Dawg, a UGA alum.

"He's here. I'll text you later."

"I need on-the-hour updates," Kiysha said. "And please check his family tree first."

Stephen jumped down from the truck. Jumped was an accurate word. At only five feet five myself, I estimated that Stephen would meet me eye to eye, but only because he was wearing a shoe that looked like it had a slight heel. First, I'd kissed my cousin and now I was about to go out with one of the kids from the Lollipop Guild in The Wizard of Oz.

Bad Vaughn. A person couldn't control their height any more than they could control their race. What Stephen lacked in height, he probably made up for with the sweetest personality. "Okay, Lord, here we go again.

Let this one be a good one," I prayed. I was about to step out of my car when my cell buzzed with a text from Trace.

Date today?

Two.

You're on a roll.

Call u ltr.

2morrow. Going out w/Stephanie.

My heart jumped and that envious feeling came over it again. Who was I to be green when I was planning on eleven more dates with random men? No commitment involved. No real chance to get my heart crushed again. Being in love with Trace scared me, but watching him fall in love with someone else could possibly scare me more.

I sighed at my thoughts. Trace wasn't out of my heart, but I couldn't hold him on a string because I was unsure of our relationship. I was unsure about *any* relationship with a man. But there was no time for thoughts of Trace now. I dropped my cell in the bottom of my purse and stepped out of my car.

"You must be Vaughn. Please tell me you're Vaughn?" Stephen crooned as soon as I walked into the restaurant. He clasped his hands together and went down on one knee.

Really?

"Yes," I said, slightly embarrassed at the spectacle he was making. "Nice to meet you, Stephen."

"Trust me," he said, finally standing up. "The pleasure is *all* mine."

Stephen had a unique look and I couldn't pin down his race or nationality, not that it particularly mattered. His hair was sandy brown and perfectly matched the freckles on his face. His eyes, a mesmerizing light grey, twinkled in the light.

The hostess approached us slowly as if she were interrupting a moment.

"We're ready to be seated," I assured her.

"Right this way." She was clearly amused, as we exchanged *that look* before she took us to our table. Stephen waited until I was seated before he sat down. A gentleman, I noted.

We both ordered sweet tea, before heading over to the buffet.

"Yo, so I've heard the buffet here is dope."

Did he say yo? And dope?

"Southern cuisine at its best," I said. "I've eaten here tons of times."

"You know they have fried chicken," he added.

I wondered if my facial expression showed what I was thinking. I didn't want to read too much into it. "I've been trying to stay away from fried foods," I said. "But for Paschal's, I'll make an exception."

"I knew you'd love the chicken. That's one reason why I chose this place."

I cleared my throat and looked around to see if anyone had eavesdropped on our conversation, but the other ravenous patrons seemed too busy navigating the line. My mouth watered. I'd only had half bagel and a cup of juice to hold me over this morning.

"I don't know about you, but I'm starving,"

"Man, it feels like my stomach is eating my back I'm so hungry," Stephen said a little too loud. His comment garnered a few chuckles behind us.

Stephen hovered behind me, walking too close for my comfort. "Let me keep it one hundred. I didn't believe you could meet me this early. I thought you'd be in church until like, two or three o'clock."

I spooned a healthy scoop of fluffy scrambled eggs and cheese grits on my plate. "Our morning service starts at nine."

"At my church, we're like in and out in an hour, but I know black churches like to stay in service all day so you can jump and shout around. I've seen the movies." Stephen dipped to the side. "You know—the choirs leaning and rocking. Club style. That's what I'm talking about. I should come to church with you one day."

If I hadn't been so hungry, I would've left him holding his serving spoon of yams. I wondered how many stereotypes and clichés he was going to throw my way by the end of this disaster. While we ate, it only took Stephen thirty minutes to use the phrases: "the blacker the berry, the sweeter the juice," and "black don't crack." I filled my belly to capacity and ignored most of his ignorant remarks. When Stephen licked his lips and told me he was "down with the brown", I decided it was time to stop being greedy and end the nonsense. The last thing I wanted to do on this beautiful Sunday was school a grown man about racial etiquette.

"I need to step out to the ladies room," I said, excusing myself and taking my purse off the back of the chair.

"I liked you when I saw you coming, but I love you when I watch you leaving," Stephen said, standing to help me out of my chair. He could watch me and my behind go straight out the door. When I noticed he was distracted with entertaining the waiter that came to refill our glasses of tea, I slipped out the front door of the restaurant and hightailed it to my car. I'd never driven so fast down Northside Drive.

Bellamy and Kiysha weren't going to believe this and I didn't feel like sharing yet another dating catastrophe.

By the evening, it was clear that my Mix & Mingle dates were a source of comedy. It turned out that I'd had to make the great escape twice in one day. I had to give it to God. He definitely had a sense of humor.

I walked in the door from my date with Carlton, stepped out of my shoes, and put my purse on the front entryway table. Somewhere, there were other single women playing the dating game and most likely losing. I had to let the cyberworld know of this foolishness. My laptop was still plugged up and on the kitchen table from Saturday night when I'd been watching YouTube videos on creative solutions on decorating a blank wall. I pulled on a pair of yellow and black striped slipper socks with the word *BUZZ* stitched across the toes. And I had plenty to buzz about. My fingers could barely keep up with my mind as I recounted every detail of my dates with Corey-Bryant, Stephen, and finally Carlton.

DATE #3

Church has always been my safe haven. I thought I'd be free of the drama but for whatever reason it followed me there. I must take part responsibility for this mess since I've refused to let any of these men have my phone number. Had I spoken to any of these men beforehand, I probably would've been able to weed out the crazy ones. But when Carlton invited me to the play at his church, I expected a quiet and solemn experience. Everyone who knows me knows that I'm a church girl....and proud of it. I'm vocal about the God I serve. And Carlton is, too. Very vocal.

It turned out that the play was about the life of Jesus and brought many of the pages of the New Testament to life. I have to admit it was touching, especially when the choir's angelic voices opened the play with one of my favorite gospel hymns. Then the play began. Carlton's first sniffles came when the pregnant Mary had to ride a donkey to Bethlehem. At first I thought he was dealing with a cold so I offered him a piece of tissue and a peppermint, both of which he accepted. Heads turned when he crumpled the plastic wrapping and crunched the peppermint until it was gone. I'd never been so relieved to be sitting in the dark, which made the bright red EXIT sign easier to see.

When the innkeeper turned away Mary and Joseph and sent them to the stable instead, Carlton began to cry a little louder. That's when I realized a cold wasn't the culprit.

His shoulders heaved up and down when the room went completely black in preparation for the birth of Jesus. Don't get me wrong...I'm all for a man having a little sensitivity. My Daddy told me there's nothing wrong with a man who is strong enough to cry. I guarantee my Daddy has never met a man like Carlton. Once the waterworks started he couldn't seem to turn them off.

"Are you okay?" I'd asked.

He blubbered something I couldn't understand. Clearly he was having issues that had nothing to do with Mary, Joseph, Baby Jesus, or the three Wise Men. I couldn't contain my laughter. It was one of those uncontrollable ones that are inappropriate for the occasion—like laughing at a funeral—but you can't stop even when you try. Carlton thought I'd become overcome with emotion, too, so he folded his arm around me and sobbed like a baby. If you think Jesus wept, you should've heard Carlton. And that was only the beginning. I still had to endure his emotional outbursts through Jesus' persecution, His Crucifixion, and His Resurrection. I'd never been so happy that Jesus rose than I had tonight.

And since Jesus rose to set us free, I took that as my sign to exit stage left.

As I clicked the button to post my blog entry, my cell rang. It was Trace.

"What's up?" he said when I answered.

"Posting some things to my blog," I said. "These fabulous dates of mine have sparked my creativity."

"Is that good or bad?"

"Depends on who's reading it. It's good for some laughs, that's for sure," I said, pulling my curtain sheers across the patio doors. I padded down the hallway and into my bedroom where I collapsed into the middle of my bed.

"That doesn't sound good. As a matter of fact I'm in front of my laptop right now. Let's see how your day has been."

"You couldn't wait, could you?" I asked.

Trace was silent for a moment and I could tell he'd already delved into my post.

"I feel responsible," he said. Despite his words, his voice didn't sound apologetic at all. In fact, he hadn't done a great job at hiding his amusement.

"You are definitely responsible," I said. "Some present. Next time, I'll take a gift card to Bloomingdales."

"Noted," Trace said. "And old boy *was* pretty loud," Trace said. "But you managed to make a graceful exit."

"And how would you know?" I asked cautiously.

"I was there. Stephanie goes to the same church and invited me to the play. We were sitting about four rows behind you," Trace admitted.

Four rows behind me but a front row seat to my humiliation, I thought. Even though I

was curious about whether Stephanie was a bombshell, I was glad I hadn't seen her. Them. Together.

"I still have nine dates to go. I'm keeping hope alive."

"You're a brave woman," Trace said. "I would've called it quits after I kissed my cousin."

"Did you have to bring that up?" I paused. I couldn't help but ask. "So who have you been kissing?"

"Does it matter to you?" Trace asked.

"Not really. I'm just curious," I lied, getting up to light the lavender scented candles around the room. I really needed a *wooosaaa* moment.

"I haven't kissed Stephanie if that's what you're asking. We've been out twice so I don't think I have a pass to slob over her face. We're getting to know each other."

For one thing, Trace had never slobbed my face. His kisses were always more calculated, sensual and tender. Heat rose in my cheeks thinking about it. Stop, it Vaughn, I told myself.

"It really only takes one date to know if you click with somebody. So what do you think about Stephanie?" I pressed, but tried to sound like it was a casual suggestion. After only a second, I wished I hadn't asked the question. I don't think I truly wanted to know.

"She's nice. Intelligent."

He stopped there. There was an awkward silence.

"Up for company?" Trace asked, tentatively.

Trace's question made me feel better. Emotions. Hormones. Whatever you want to call them, they were crazy. One minute I pushed Trace away and the next minute I wanted to hang on to what we once had. But all good things must come to an end, so I had to end our relationship before I was left holding the pieces to another broken heart. At least I knew that Stephanie hadn't completely stolen him away from me.

I glanced at the clock on my end table. 9:24. Even if Trace walked out the door at this exact second, by the time he made it to my place it would almost be ten o'clock at night. I was feeling lonely, so that was a dangerous combination.

"It's pretty late. Let's catch up later this week," I suggested.

"Right. I know how hard it is for you to keep your hands off of me," he teased. "I'm working from home this week so the ball's in your court," he said. "Let me know when you can pencil me in between your other men."

"Speaking of other men, I'm meeting some guy named Harold tomorrow. We're grabbing lunch. I figure it's an easy way to get in and get out if it's another bomb," I said.

"Nobody's making you go on these dates. You *can* choose not to respond to these emails you're getting."

"Twelve dates is what I'm supposed to have, so twelve dates is what I'm going to do," I said. "Actually, at least ten. Kiysha and I have a bet."

"I don't even want to know," Trace said. "The two of you can come up with some crazy stuff."

"My dollhouse is on the line," I told him. Trace knew how much I adored the dollhouse that had a special place in the corner of my guest bedroom.

"Then it looks like you're stuck in it," Trace decided.

"Three down, seven to go. I'll write about Harold as soon as I can."

"And I'll be the first to read it. Sweet dreams, Vee," Trace said. He used to call me Vee all the time even though I loved my full birth name so much that I'd never let anyone shorten it with a nickname. No one, except Trace.

Chapter 6

I could hear the words to my blog post forming in my head as soon as I walked up to Harold. He was mature, in this case the politically correct, word for saying old. But at least he was handsome in an Eddie Levert sort of way. He was easy to imagine dancing choreographed moves in a line up of old school R&B Crooners like The Whispers or The Pips. In a lot of ways, he reminded me of my stepfather, Philip, the man I had affectionately named Jazzy P. Jazzy P was my mom's fourth husband and my third stepfather.

This was sure to be a date to remember and I was more relieved than ever that I'd informed Harold in my email that I was only available for an hour.

"Harold?" I said, approaching him when I noticed the single rose he told me he'd be carrying. "I'm Vaughn."

"Nice to see you. Glad you could make it, baby girl,"

Harold said, handing me the long stem. "For you."

"How sweet." I put my nose close to the yellow petals and tried not to comment on the fact that he'd already given me a pet name. I would've corrected him, but I felt more inclined to respect my elders.

He led me into Prime, the top rated steak, sushi and seafood restaurant in Lenox Mall where we were promptly seated. It was no surprise that our service and meal were top notch, but even more pleasant about the experience was Harold. He was insightful about the movers and shakers in Atlanta and when the time ticked past my allotted hour, I told him I could rearrange my schedule. He looked pleased. There wasn't a single bone in my body that was remotely attracted to Harold, and I think he felt the same about me. We were simply good company for each other.

If I were to choose a man on looks alone, Harold would pass the test. He had thick salt and pepper hair and a full beard that he'd groomed low to his face. I could tell he'd been raised in an era when chivalry was the rule, not the exception. His voice was deep and sultry, perfect for late night radio and I found a certain fatherly comfort in spending time with him.

"It seems like the older some of these women get, the shorter their hemlines and the lower their bust lines get," Harold whispered, when we passed a woman wearing an outfit more appropriate for a woman twenty years younger. Harold and I had decided to stroll around the mall for a little window shopping.

"Isn't that what men these days like?" I said, resisting the urge to turn around and catch a behind-the-scenes view of the woman who'd teetered past us.

"Most men are going to look," Harold said, "but that's not what they want forever. It's a temporary thing. I'm too old for temporary. Give me forever or give me nothing."

"If you don't mind me asking, what attracted you to attend the Mix & Mingle Matchmakers event? It's obvious most of the women there were—," I paused, trying not to offend him.

"Too young for me?" Harold asked. I stopped with him to admire a gray, three-piece suit in a store window. "For every older man who wants a young woman, there's a young woman who prefers an older man. Trust me on that one."

He smiled wide enough for me to see that he probably had most of his original teeth.

"Besides, age is all in the mind. Maybe a little in my achy knees every now and then, but definitely more mental for me," he joked. "I feel young. I'm in excellent health, and I want to settle down with a younger woman who's not opposed to having children. At least one."

"You want children?" I asked incredulously. "Really?" As fatherly as Harold seemed to be, I couldn't imagine him changing dirty diapers or taking the late night shift for upset tummies and teething troubles when he was clearly old enough to count down the days until retirement.

"I've always wanted children." Harold said. "But my first wife was never able to conceive and she wasn't comfortable with adopting. Instead, we poured all of our love and attention on our nieces and nephews. I've always wanted my own son to carry on my legacy and my name. I think most men do. And like I said, I'm healthy physically. I've had everything examined and tested. Everything. It's not too late, yet. One of the contractors who worked on my house was fifty-nine when he had his last baby. His wife was forty-four. It might be rare, but it's possible. All I need is one strong swimmer." He stuffed his hands in his pockets and we started walking again. "Pardon me for being so blunt."

"So you only want a young wife so she can bear your children?" I questioned, finding his reasoning intriguing and slightly chauvinistic.

"Absolutely not. I want a wife for companionship. For love. I want a wife because God says it's not good for man to be alone. Don't you know a man who finds a wife finds favor with the Lord?"

"Yes, sir," I said. "That's what the Bible says."

"Please call me Harold," he said. "You've been calling me sir since we started eating."

"I didn't even realize it," I said. "I was always taught to respect my elders." I flinched. "Look, he said. "I never deny the truth. I'm old enough to be your father." He pinched my cheek. "But young enough to be your Big Daddy."

"I can't bear to call you Big Daddy," I said, walking into Banana Republic. I hadn't taken offense to his comment at all since I knew he had a sense of humor. "I like Huggy Bear better."

"I don't know whether to take that as a compliment or not," Harold laughed.

"It's definitely a compliment. You're like a snuggly toy to take to bed to feel warm and safe."

Harold lifted his brows at me and it took me a second to realize the double meaning of my words.

"That wasn't meant to be a proposition," I hurried to clarify. "My Promised Land is closed and locked and can only be opened with the two words."

"I do?"

"Exactly," I said.

Harold held his hand open and I slapped a high-five in his wide palm.

"I could tell you were different from the first time I sent you an email and you refused to give me your phone number. To me, that means you're a woman who knows your worth."

"Thank you," I said. I searched through a rack of black slacks—as if I actually needed another pair—while Harold kept holding up blouses that he thought fit my fashion taste. I had to admit he was right on the nose. Either he'd been hanging around enough women to know what worked best for their bodies, or he had a natural knack for style. Probably the latter. After all, he was wearing a pair of trendy jeans and a graphic t-shirt with studs on the front. The studs matched the ones that ran along the stitching on his leather shoes. I knew quality shoes when I saw them.

"Go ahead and pick something out," Harold said. "My treat."

It was tempting, but there was no way I'd Harold let buy me anything besides lunch.

"Absolutely not," I said. "I can handle it." I carried an emerald green blouse with Victorian style sleeves into the wardrobe room. Harold settled onto a leather bench outside of the dressing room area while I tried on the blouse. "You know this blouse looks even better on than it does on the hanger," I called out to him. "You have a great sense of style. Not too bad for an old man," I joked.

There was no answer from Harold. Knowing him, he'd gone back out to the floor and struck up a conversation with one of the associates to see if any of them minded being with a man with more years behind him than in front of him. I still couldn't believe Harold wanted to have children at his age. At this point, even if he married a woman tomorrow and she got pregnant immediately, Harold would be in his late sixties before his child started kindergarten. That would definitely cause some confusion at school on Grandparents Day, I thought as I changed back into my crisp white button down. If God could do it for Abraham, who was I to think that He wouldn't perform the same miracle for Harold?

I swept a comb through hair and freshened up my peach lipstick. I stopped in mid-step when I noticed Harold still in his chair, but slumped over on his side. My heart leaped into my throat.

"Harold?" I attempted to lift his shoulder so I could see his face, but his awkward position made it hard to do so.

"Oh, my God!" I panicked. "Harold!" I shook him violently. No response. Where was everyone? I pressed my fingers on the vein on the side of his throat to see if I could detect a pulse, then realized that I had absolutely no idea what I was doing. Calm down, Vaughn, I told myself. Think.

I ran out into the store to find assistance. Somebody. Anybody.

"I need help! Somebody call 9-1-1!"

A nearby female associate ran into the wardrobe area with me. "Oh, Jesus. What happened?" she asked, stepping away from him like it was a murder scene. She looked back at me with terror in her eyes.

"I don't know. I found him like this when I came out of the dressing room." I dumped the contents of my purse on the floor so I could find my cell phone.

The associate fell to her knees and laid her face against Harold's. I assumed she was trying to detect his breathing, but she looked as distraught as I felt.

"What should I do?" She was almost in tears.

Suddenly Harold pushed himself up like he was on the end of a puppeteer string. "How about finding that blouse in a size 6?"

I jumped back. Frightened. Confused. I used to say I wanted to witness a miracle like someone being raised from the dead, but at that exact moment I changed my mind. My heart probably couldn't take it without dying myself.

"You've got to be kidding me!" I said, punching his shoulder. Once. Twice. Three times. "That was cruel."

"It may have been cruel, but it sure was funny," Harold said. He kneeled down and helped me put the contents back in my purse, while the sales associate disappeared back onto the sales floor. The poor woman was probably horrified.

He opened his arms wide when he realized that I'd genuinely been upset. "Huggy Bear is sorry," he said, pulling me into arms.

"Your new name is Grizzly Bear. A Huggy Bear wouldn't do that."

"My wife always used to tell me that my practical jokes went too far."

We walked to the front so I could purchase my blouse. In the midst of all the mayhem, I'd almost forgotten my fashionable find. I wouldn't have minded finding some accessories to complement it, but it since I was supposed to meet clients within the hour, I'd have to pass. Even though the house I was showing them was only twenty minutes away, I didn't trust Atlanta traffic.

"Are you going to let me buy that for you now?" Harold asked.

"Absolutely," I said, throwing out my prior hesitation. "You owe it to me now."

Harold shoved his hand in his pocket and pulled out a handful of peppermints. He took one for himself and offered one to me. I accepted Harold's offer—in case it was his indirect way of telling me that my after-lunch breath needed refreshing. With bag in hand, Harold and I walked back into the bustle of mall shoppers. The scent of mocha coffee and cinnamon buns floated through the air. The aromas reminded me of Christmas and made me want to go into another baking binge.

"Well, baby girl," Harold said, slipping a Bluetooth piece into his ear. "It looks like our time is up. But I must say I thoroughly enjoyed your company. You're a gem. Whatever man finds you will find a treasure."

"Thank you very much," I said. "And the woman you will find will be blessed beyond measure. No matter how old she is," I added with a smile.

Harold handed the valet our tickets. I was glad I'd chosen to valet since a mist hovered over the air and I'd left my umbrella in my car.

"There are two things I always tell my nieces," Harold said while we waited. "Look for the man who will give you three if he has four. Look for the man who wants the best for you more than he wants it for himself. That's the kind of man you deserve, Ms. Vaughn."

Okay, maybe it was the mist outside that was clouding my eyes. I'm not sappy. I'm not typically the woman who cries during chick flicks or wallows for hours when a relationship ends. But Huggy Bear had brought a little tear to my eye. He handed me a business card as a jet black two door convertible coupe—with 22-inch rims—circled through the valet. I wondered what celebrity was coming to drop thousands in shopping this time.

"That's me," Harold said. "I know you like to stay incognito, but call me if you ever need anything."

I looked at Harold's business card for the first time. He owned a luxury car dealership in Buckhead. I prayed he didn't hook up with a woman during this whole Mix & Mingle ordeal who wanted him for his money and not his heart, but I had the feeling that he'd be able to tell the difference.

Harold opened the door and I got a peek of his customized interior with the monogrammed headrest.

"I guess young blood really does run through your veins," I said.

He tapped the side of his head with his index finger. "It's all a state of mind."

"You'll definitely hear from me again," I said. "Thank you for lunch, the blouse, *and* your wisdom."

"Anytime," he said. He handed two bills to the valet who'd driven his car up. "That's for me and the young lady."

Finally, a date that I left me refreshed instead of embarrassed. Harold was an oldie but goodie.

Chapter 7

Bellamy and Kiysha entered my front door in full Atlanta Braves regalia. One of Bellamy's clients had given her tickets for prime seats, but I'd passed on her offer. I preferred indoor arenas and was willing to hold out for fifty-yard line seats for the Falcons or half-court seats for the Hawks. Besides, the weather had taken a turn, and as was typical of spring, had been rainy overnight. Scattered showers were expected to move through later, and I wasn't enough of a fan of any athletic team to get drenched.

"Whoop, whoop!" Kiysha said, pumping her fists as she marched around my living room. "We are in the prime seats and I can't wait to see the prime rib on the diamond."

"Is she talking about what I think she's talking about?" Bellamy asked.

"The best selection of beef to be found," Kiysha said.

"People underestimate baseball players all the time, but they are some cuties. I checked them out on the Braves website."

"I promise. One of these days we're going to have some serious prayer for you," Bellamy said.

"I tell you all the time she needs Jesus. And by the way your hair looks so cute like that," I said, admiring the way Bellamy had molded it back behind her ears instead of wearing it full and fluffy.

"Are you sure? This cut is supposed to be the new trend in Hollywood but it hasn't really been working out for me. What was I thinking when I cut my hair, especially before the wedding?"

"Hollywood or not, be your own trendsetter," Kiysha said. "I do my own thing."

"Obviously," I said, taking her in from head to toe. She was wearing an old Chipper Jones baseball jersey that she'd slashed on the sides. At least she was wearing a t-shirt underneath since the jersey hugged her silhouette like spandex. The bottom of Kiysha's black skinny jeans disappeared inside of a pair of red leather combat boots. As if that wasn't enough, her earrings look liked huge feathers that swept across her shoulders. It was a big contrast to Bellamy who was dressed more conservatively in boot cut jeans with a blue Braves t-shirt, baseball cap and tennis shoes. My two besties were like night and day.

"So what are your plans for tonight?" Bellamy asked

me. "Another blind date? I loved that post you wrote about Huggy Bear. He seemed sweet. I want to squeeze him."

"He was definitely squeezable," I said. I plopped down on the pillows I'd propped around the coffee table. For the last hour I'd been working on a one thousand piece jigsaw puzzle of the New York cityscape. I'd read that puzzles were supposed to be relaxing, but those first fifty or so pieces I'd put together had been frustrating. "Trace is coming over so no dates for me until tomorrow. A guy named Roy sent me an email." I scrolled through my inbox and handed Bellamy the phone so she could read the message:

"*Ready for a challenge? Meet me on Tuesday at 3.*"

"Where's the address to?" Bellamy asked.

"I looked it up. It's to a bowling and arcade center."

"First of all, who plans a date like that in the middle of the day?" Kiysha asked from the kitchen where she was surveying the food options in my refrigerator. "Wait a minute. I know. I man without a J-O-B. I say save your time and skip it."

I shrugged, even though I'd had the same thought. "My schedule happens to be open. He probably has an awkward work schedule." I snapped a puzzle piece into place. "Besides, he has no idea that I play a mean Ms. Pac-Man game. If he wants a challenge at the arcade, I'll give him one."

Evidently Kiysha didn't find anything in my fridge to

her liking. She came to the couch, flipped open her compact and applied bright red lip gloss to her full lips. She popped her lips together then checked her teeth for smudges. "Then it should be fun and definitely blog-worthy." she decided. "Reading your blog is my highest source of entertainment right now, but my biggest concern is that you're being safe. You know the drill. Call or text us when you get there and keep us posted."

"Don't worry. I'm still keeping my full name a secret, and in case I happen upon a cuckoo, I keep my Taser close at hand."

I hadn't had to use my Taser yet, but it supposedly issued enough voltage to bring a grown man to his knees. For my sake, I hoped it was true. I'd shock a man in one breath, but pray for him in the next.

Kiysha dropped her makeup bag back in her purse. "I almost forgot. I have a little something for you in case these dates bring the gift of romance in your life. Or if you want a reason to do some lip-locking with your real man, Trace."

She pulled her hand out of her purse, producing a sprig of fake mistletoe.

"Seriously? Who uses mistletoe in April?"

"You can use all the help you can get," Kiysha said. "But make sure you don't go dangling this thing over the heads of any more of your relatives."

I swatted at it but she snatched it out of my reach before I could send it flying across the room. Not counting Bryant, the last man I kissed was Trace. And now all of a sudden my mind was on him. And his lips. And the amazing times we always had together. The phone conversations that lasted long into the night. And the fact that he was on his way over right now and I couldn't wait to see him.

As if on cue, the doorbell rang. It was Trace. That always happened with him. Bellamy stood up "That's our sign to leave. You two have fun. Keep it clean and kick him out if it looks like things would get hot and heavy."

I held up my empty ring finger. "Nothing going down without a ring and a wedding. And like I've said hundreds of times. We are friends," I insisted.

"As you should be," Kiysha said. "Friends make the best lovers. Couples who are friends first last forever. These other dates are a total waste of time in my opinion."

"Nice try. But you're not making me lose the bet."

"I still can't believe you put your dollhouse on the line." Bellamy said.

"Dang," Kiysha said. "I've lost my touch. I used to be able to convince you to do anything."

"That was when we were six," I said, laughing. "Times have changed."

Kiysha held the mistletoe over my head, then kissed me on the cheek. "Talk to you later, girlie. Don't forget to write a blog post about your arcade date tomorrow. I sent a link to your blog to every woman I know."

"Which explains my sudden increase in subscribers," I said. Before my post about Huggy Bear I had about twenty, but this afternoon there were one hundred and three. I guess the dating game was one many women played.

"See you later, boo," Bellamy said.

When Bellamy swung open my door, Trace was standing in the doorway with an armful of red roses and a box of Krispy Kreme doughnuts.

"Isn't he so sweet?" Kiysha said with a grin. "Trace wants to fatten you up for the next man."

"Good-bye, Kiysha," Trace said. "Be on your best behavior."

"That's what I should be telling you," she said, taking a sniff of the roses as she walked by.

Trace pushed the door closed with his foot and I slid the doughnut box out of his hand before he had the chance to offer it to me.

"This is so wrong, but so right." I sank my teeth into the warmth of my first doughnut, licking the sweet glaze from the corner of my mouth. Trace and I had a history so I knew this box of a dozen would be empty and stuffed in the trash by the end of the night. I could hear Helene's voice encouraging me to come back to her spin class at the gym. Trace had a gym in his basement that he used on a daily basis, and I knew he'd work on his abs during his workout. I hadn't seen *them* since our trip to the beach last summer but I was sure *they* were still there.

"Since when did you start doing puzzles?" he asked, passing by my new project.

"My way to relax today."

"Is it working?" he said, going into the kitchen. He looked under the kitchen sink where I kept the empty vases from the countless flower arrangements he'd brought for me. Unexpected flowers, he said, made a woman smile. It made her feel special, just because. He was right.

"Beautiful roses," I said.

"Beautiful woman," he replied. Trace opened the side drawer for a pair of shearing scissors.

"Is this your attempt to apologize for my disastrous dates?" I asked. "They're all your fault, you know."

"Don't blame me." Trace said with a slight chuckle. "You might have made a bet with Kiysha, but you're curious, too."

He was right. Curiosity kept me answering the emails from these men. "Some of us haven't been lucky enough to have a colleague introduce us to someone. Does Shandra know you're here?"

"We're not a couple. It doesn't matter if *Stephanie* knows where I am," correcting me even though her name was already fused in my mind. "She's in New York for a few days. I dropped her off at the airport this morning."

I wanted this conversation to stop. Even though I hadn't given a second thought to sharing my dating adventures with him, I didn't like to hear him talk about another woman.

"Oh, you did? It seems like her company would've sent a car to take her."

"They were going to, but I offered."

He kept his attention on arranging the roses and I pretended to be more concerned with pouring myself a tall glass of milk. Maybe it would help wash down some of this envy.

I studied Trace while he slipped the roses into the vase one-by-one. Most women saw him as the total package, and there was no denying that he had more going for him that he had against him. But even the most handsome, intelligent, and financially stable men had their quirks. I absent-mindedly bit into my second doughnut. Trace was no different. There was no such thing as perfection in a person. I could admit that. But many things surfaced once couples said "I do." I saw that in my mother's marriages. Thankfully for her, she'd struck gold with Jazzy P, but I couldn't endure three failed marriages before I found the one to last forever.

Marriage was hard work. Sometimes the dating stopped, the monthly vases of roses withered, and the slight disagreements became full-blown arguments. What was the point of committing to a marriage that had a fifty percent chance of ending anyway?

"So where's the spread?" Trace asked after he'd finished perfecting the flower arrangement. He positioned the vase on the middle of my kitchen table, washed his hands, and then ate an entire doughnut in two bites.

"I had a full afternoon," I said. "I'm so thankful I decided to go ahead and show that house today because my clients decided to put in a bid. If I have a closing this month, that's going to set me up nice for some birthday spending cash. I haven't decided what I want to do yet. Maybe I'll go away for the weekend for a getaway before I jump back into work."

"That'll be nice," Trace said, distracted with looking through my take-out menus. "Wings or Chinese?"

"Whatever you want. I'm not that hungry. I'm still pretty full from lunch."

"I can't tell," Trace said, closing the doughnut box.

"Some things are an exception," I said. "Especially Krispy Kreme."

I popped him on the back of his head.

"Love taps," he said, and opened up the take out menu for the China Express down the street.

"I'm good with some lo mein noodles, vegetables, and a couple of spring rolls," he said, assessing the list of dinner combinations. "Are you sure you don't want anything?"

I'd been staring at him and didn't realize it.

"I wouldn't mind some clam chowder from that deli I like, but that's in the opposite direction from the Chinese spot," I said, thinking about stashing something for dinner tomorrow.

"No problem. I don't mind. No salad?"

"I guess I should," I said. "Get me a –"

"Caesar salad with extra croutons and the dressing in a container on the side." He winked at me.

My heart fluttered and I looked away.

Trace picked up my keys and the key card for the building. "I don't want to lose my visitor's spot," he said. "I'll be circling the block forever if I do. You might want to consider buying one of those fancy houses you're always selling. Then you wouldn't have to worry about parking when you have company over."

"But I'll have to worry about roof repairs, lawn maintenance, a random leaky pipe, and cleaning up rooms I'd probably never go into."

"If you were my woman you wouldn't have to worry about those things."

"And if I were your wife, I'd be wearing aprons and house slippers instead of Dana Buchman and Michael Kors. And instead of writing up contracts for six-figure houses, I'd have to cook breakfast, pack your lunch, and have your hot dinner on the table every evening."

"Vee, I didn't say if you were my *wife*, I said if you were my *woman*. Your mind took it to another level so it must be somewhere in your mind. And as far as you being my wife and personal chef, you know that's not true either."

"It's definitely true," I said, going back to my point.

"That's what your mom does for your dad, and we all know the apple doesn't fall far from the tree. You couldn't have imagined your mother working outside of the home because she was there for you for everything. All the time."

"Yes, I grew up accustomed to seeing certain things, but that doesn't mean that's the way it *has* to be for me. Would I like to have a wife who stayed at home? Yes, eventually. I think. But that shouldn't matter to you because you've made it clear where we stand."

"Trace. You know how I feel about you. I've loved you. I *do* love you."

"But not enough to accept my proposal. Not enough to be my wife." He exhaled. I could tell he was frustrated by the way his eyebrows creased in the middle of his forehead.

"It's complicated. Marriage isn't easy."

"My parents have been married for thirty-two years. I know it's not easy. They haven't tried to paint their life as a fairy tale. I've heard the arguments behind closed doors. Seen the tears. But they never gave up.

Trace shoved my key ring into his pocket and headed towards the door. "I'll be back." He turned one last time before going out. "You're Vaughn Holiday, not Meta Holiday-

Simms. You don't have to do it three times to get it right."

I picked up a pair of socks from my basket and threw

it at him. Had he not blocked it with his hands I would've hit a bullseye in his mouth. The mood lightened.

"I'm telling. I promise I will call Meta Holiday-Simms right now and tell her what you said."

"You can't fault me for speaking the truth," Trace said. "But go ahead and call her. She'll be on my side."

"It's sad to say you're right," I agreed. In my mom's eyes, Trace could do no wrong. In the six months since I'd turned down Trace's proposal, I'd yet to talk to my mom about it detail. She'd pressed the situation, but I'd never given in. She'd known about Trace's proposal even before I did, because doing the proper thing, Trace had called and asked her for permission.

"I'll be back," Trace said.

You've never left, I thought to myself.

Chapter 8

All the talk about my mom reminded me that I'd missed making my usual Monday morning call to her. I picked up the house phone that I rarely used. I'd spoken to her briefly after she and Jazzy P returned from their vacation to Hawaii, but I'd skipped updating her about Bryant. She'd want to know how we crossed paths in the first place, and I hadn't planned on telling her about my Mix and Mingle dates. She'd frown on the whole idea, not only because she was leery of blind dates, but because she was Trace's number one cheerleader.

I could imagine her now traipsing around the house all bronzed and carefree after a week of wading in the North Pacific Ocean. The trip was their celebratory vacation for being empty nesters. After taking a year off to "find herself," my sister, Oopsie, had finally started her freshman year at UCLA in the fall.

Years ago, my parents started their empty nester

countdown when I entered my freshman year in high school. Apparently they'd reveled so much in their impending freedom that my mother ended up pregnant. From the time she walked out of the bathroom with the white pregnancy test in hand, we'd started calling the baby, Oopsie.

"Hello, Mother," I said, yelling over the gospel music blaring in the background.

"Hold on a minute, Vaughn. Let me turn down the music. I'm having church up in here." Last Christmas I'd given my mother an iPod with a dock station and Bluetooth speakers. As an extra bonus, I'd downloaded and transferred nearly every piece of music I owned so that she'd stop buying bootleg gospel CDs from her "hookup" at the beauty salon.

"Now," she crooned when she came back to the phone. "Hey, baby. It's about time you called."

"Mother, the phone works both ways," I said.

"I know, but I'm the parent. *You're* supposed to call *me.*"

The Queen was now back on her throne. "Whatever makes you happy," I said. My mother had always had rules that applied specifically to her. She called them her parent privileges. She loved quoting the verse in the Bible about children honoring their parents so they'd live a long time. And because I wanted to live as long as possible, I usually kept my mouth shut. "What are you up to?" I asked her.

"Unpacking, so I can wash and repack."

"Did you say repack?"

"Yesssss," she sang. "My honey is taking me away again. In two weeks. But you know how I like to be ahead of the game."

"Where are you going this time?" I said, opening new packages of the lavender scented air fresheners I kept strategically placed around the room.

"It's a surprise, sweetheart. That's the most romantic part of it. And I'm going to sit back and be on my best behavior and not try to figure out where we're going."

"I don't believe you," I said. My mother was a classic Type A personality. Being in control was in her DNA.

"I'm telling the truth. I'm taking my cues from you. You said you were going to let loose and not work so much for a few weeks, so I'm going to do something different, too. I'm not going to be a control freak. Personally, I don't see how I'm that controlling, but since everybody says it—" she cleared her throat—"I'm going to work on myself in that area."

"I'm proud of you, Mom."

"Self-reflection. We've all got to do it. We'll be better off for it. You make sure you're looking at the woman in the mirror while you're on this work sabbatical thing you've got going on."

"I will," I promised. I heard the dryer timer buzz in the background, followed by a lot of clanking with what sounded like my mother unloading the dryer and reloading it with freshly washed clothes.

"You won't believe what I did," she said after a moment.

"You're scaring me," I said. The last time she said something like that, she'd taken a pole dancing class for seniors. Strictly for exercise, she'd claimed, but I'd yet to get that visual of my mother out of my head.

"I bought a bikini," my mother blurted out.

I thought I'd only groaned in my head, but evidently I hadn't.

"What's that for? Gravity may have taken its toll in some places, but I'm not bad looking. I'm not the best, but I'm definitely not the worse. Trust me. I saw all shapes and sizes when we were in Hawaii. People who should've been ashamed, but weren't."

My mother was a petite, but shapely woman. She still had the goods and I prayed God and genetics would be gracious to me in the same way. At sixty-two years old, she went to her local gym for water aerobics twice a week and even caught the occasional Zumba class. She embraced her age and would proudly whip out her AARP card. That was the only thing she should whip out as far as I was concerned.

"So did you just buy the bikini, or have you worn it yet?"

"I wore it, but with a cover up. At least out on the beach, but not at the hotel."

I stopped my mother before she went *there*. There

are some conversations that a mother and daughter shouldn't have.

"You're too much. I have to make sure I pray for Jazzy P every day."

"Please do. We both need all the prayer we can get."

I walked over to smell the roses on the table. I never tired of a gorgeous vase of flowers, and had always used blooms to brighten my space. From the time Trace and I had started dating, I didn't have to take my usual trip to the farmer's market for freshly cut flowers. Trace kept my home adorned with them. Roses, tulips, irises, sunflowers, lilies, orchids. Even carnations with their simplicity, lightened my mood.

"What are you having for dinner tonight?" my mom asked out of the blue.

"I had a heavy lunch, so not much if anything."

"No doughnuts? I thought Trace brought over doughnuts."

"So you've been talking to Trace, I see."

"He called me this morning, but I missed his call. When I called him back, he happened to be on his way to your house," she said, the thrill coating her voice.

"Do you think it's a good idea for you to talk to my ex-boyfriend? It leaves a door open."

"The door should be open," my mother said. "I don't see why you closed it in the first place. You know you have a history of running away good men."

"That's not true."

"It is true. Tell the truth and shame the devil. The only one who didn't deserve you was that idiot, Roderick. But every dog has his day."

That's my past."

"And Trace can be your future. There aren't many men who'll wait around, especially one like Trace, who could probably have any woman he wanted. He's got faith, he's got vision, he's got good looks, and he's got money. Don't wait until he falls in love with someone else before you come to your senses. It'll be too late then."

Why did our conversations always come back around to Trace? I'd been giving him enough thoughts of my own without her planting seeds. But Trace wasn't sitting around twiddling his fingers. There was Stephanie.

"Have you talked to Oopsie?" I asked, changing the subject. I knew that would send my mother into a tizzy and take the spotlight off of me. She'd gone off to UCLA and been fully swept off into the college life, even opting to stay in Los Angeles and spend Christmas with her roommate instead of going home to Denver. She'd texted me pictures. Oopsie's face was fuller from the freshmen fifteen she'd immediately gained and she'd chopped off all of her hair from shoulder length to a short pixie cut with highlighted tips. I loved it. Mom hated it. Jazzy P was indifferent.

"Oopsie has forgotten she has a family. She never answers when I call and when I leave a message it takes two days for her to call me back." She huffed.

Now I regretted getting my mom flustered.

"Don't take it personally. She does the same thing to me."

"You didn't act this elusive when you went off to college."

"We're two different people," I explained. "I was clingy. She's not. She's always been independent and leaving home has given her the wings she always wanted. Once the newness wears off she'll be sitting at your feet letting you comb her hair again."

"What hair?"

"Right. Well change is good."

"Not this change. Most of her friends are older and have their own apartments," my mother said. "I don't like that."

"If Oopsie is going to do something wrong, she'll do it whether she's in her dorm room or the apartment. The place doesn't matter, but the person does. Oopsie's not like that. She's got a good head on her shoulders."

"The only thing I can do is pray for my girls. Me and Patrick pray for you two all the time. I hope you know that."

"I know you do," I said. I'd stood on the wings of my mom's prayers for years. They'd not only offered practical advice, but spiritual wisdom also. And I rarely admitted it to her, but my mother was usually right when it came to my love and relationships. I guessed she'd failed enough on her own to know the red flags.

Trace's cell phone rang from somewhere in the room. I knew it was his because he never changed his ringtone from the chirp that started low, then escalated to a shrill. I followed the sound to the bar counter. It was Stephanie.

The jealous and insecure parts of me wanted to answer, but what good would it serve?

"What is that noise? Is your fire alarm going off? Are you burning something?"

"Umm. No," I said, realizing that I'd shut off everything my mom had been talking about. "It's Trace's cell."

"A man who leaves his cell phone behind clearly has nothing to hide."

"I doubt he realized it. He practically keeps this phone glued to his side for work."

The icon and alert popped up for a message. I knew Trace's passcode. It was what every security expert warned people not to use—his birthdate. I could easily listen to the message and erase it like she'd never left one. Even the most hi-tech smartphones had glitches. I wasn't the kind of woman who'd do that, but I knew one who would. I smiled. I wished Kiysha was here.

I listened to my mom ramble about the letter from the family reunion committee that was supposed to be being mailed out to everyone. My seventy-five year-old cousin had taken charge of the organizing and instead of sending emails, she sent snail mail. And although electronic payments would be more convenient, she wanted insisted everyone mail their check or money order.

I rushed my mom off the phone when I heard the door lock click. Trace was juggling the bag from the sandwich shop but also had two drinks tucked under his arm—a ginger ale for me and one of those fancy Peruvian waters for himself. I felt a shift in the room when he walked in. A warmth. A peaceful familiarity. But I brushed it off. Mom had pumped him into my head— talked him up and tried to push him back into that tiny space in my heart.

Trace looked at me like he wanted to say, *"Hello, honey. I'm home."*

Chapter 9

There's a kid in all of us. The one that falls back in the snow to make angels in the winter's first snowfall or the one that wants to lick the cake batter off the beaters from the mixer. From time to time on Saturday mornings, I even enjoyed a cartoon flashback and watched old episodes of The Flintstones and Grape Ape. But there's such a thing as taking childishness to the extreme. That was my first thought when I saw Roy on Tuesday.

Roy met me in the front of the arcade with a huge gap-toothed smile, wearing a backpack. Yes, a backpack.

"So are you in school?" I asked casually as he loaded $10 worth of credits on my playing card. Evidently he planned for this to be a short date. At these places ten dollars didn't last long.

"No," he said, patting the straps of his bag. "Snacks. They charge you an arm and a leg for a bag of chips and a drink, but I got smart. So if you get hungry, let me know. I even put some extra in here in case I see some people who look hungry. I'll sell my chips for fifty cent a bag."

"Right," I mumbled.

I could tell this was going to be a mistake, but foolishly I followed him inside. I had no idea who he'd plan on selling the chips to since it seemed that we were the only people in the building besides the employees. At least the man was financially independent and thought like an entrepreneur, I told myself. There were other ways to describe it, but my devotion this morning was about keeping a positive attitude in the midst of trials. This, although minute, was a trial.

In my head, I'd already begun writing my blog post about this Mix and Mingle date titled, "It's A Boy's World." This was going to be a good one. With my first check this morning, I'd seen a jump to five hundred and thirty-three subscribers to my blog. Evidently there had been something alluring about Harold, aka Huggy Bear.

"This is the best time to come," Roy said, handing me the card. "You don't have to wait in line for the best games and there's nobody hawking you from behind wishing you'd hurry up and finish." Roy looked hypnotized by the room full of flashing neon lights and carnival-sounding music.

"So how often do you come?" I asked, not really interested, but digging for content.

"Twice a week. Tuesdays and Thursdays."

"Every week?" I asked, incredulously.

"Every week."

I was astonished to say the least. What kind of grown man had that kind of time on his hands? There had to be a reason for it. Maybe he was a video game designer or specialized in computer animation. This was research for him—a continuing education of sorts. It had to be.

"So where do you want to start?" Roy asked me. He clasped his hands in front of his chest and rocked back and forth on the soles of his overly priced athletic shoes.

Nothing in the room looked familiar. I was used to one joystick or steering wheels but everything looked like something out of Star Wars. Too many buttons. Large automatic weapons attached to the games by thick black cords. Life-sized motorcycles and jet skis.

"I play a mean Ms. Pac Man," I finally said. "Do they have one?"

"Okay. Old school. That stuff is this way," Roy said, taking off to the left without me.

I pulled out my cell phone and took a picture of Roy from behind. I sent the image—with no words—to Kiysha. She texted back almost immediately.

Is that a backpack?

Indeed.

Whoa.

Whoa is not the word.

"Over here," Roy yelled out from where he'd disappeared into a small alcove where they'd arranged all of the video games I'd played when I was little. Ms. Pac Man, Donkey Kong, Frogger, Centipede. They seemed so archaic compared to the games up front, but it brought back memories of times with Auntie Bonnie and...*ugghh*...Bryant. I needed to call him so we could deal with the embarrassment of this situation and move past it. Later.

"This is my girl," I said. I patted the side of the Ms. Pac Man game.

"Ladies, first," Roy said, stepping out of the way.

I slid my card through the reader and the machine came alive. I flew Ms. Pac-Man through the maze, chomping pellets at record speed and eating the monsters when they turned blue. When they changed back to their original colors I dodged them with quick flicks and twists of my wrist. I hadn't lost my touch.

"Alright, alright," Roy said, obviously impressed. "You've got skills." He moved and dodged his body in sync with mine. I was really sucked into the nostalgia of it all. I chomped cherries, lemons, ate energizer pellets and gained extra lives until my turn finally came to an end almost fifteen minutes later. I rubbed my right wrist and flexed my fingers.

"I might've gotten a little carried away," I said.

"No such thing," Roy said. He almost pushed me out of the way so he could swipe his card through the reader. "Let me show you how a pro does it."

The 'pro' lost his first Ms. PacMan within thirty

seconds. Roy jiggled the controller stick.

"I think you broke this thing. It's sticking."

I shook my head. "So you want to blame me for your lack of skills." It was—literally—all fun and games to me, but Roy didn't take too kindly to it.

"Whatever," he said.

I was laughing inside. He's the one who'd sent me the message to ask if I was up for a challenge. Surely he didn't think I'd back down. If nothing else, I was a pro at talking trash. From playing endless spades games with Trace, he'd taught me how to shake a man's confidence.

Within five minutes Roy's turn was over.

I smirked. "Evidently you're not a lady's man."

Roy lifted his backpack off of his shoulders and dropped it at his feet. He swiped his card again, skipping my next turn altogether.

"There's no need to be offended about it," I said. I looked around in case this guy started to go ballistic. The only person I saw was a young redhead girl who looked about half my height, half my weight, and half my age. I searched for my lipstick Taser in the small satchel I'd brought inside and slid it into the back pocket of my jeans.

"It's only a game," I said when Roy lost another Ms. Pac-Man. He kicked the console.

Roy's nostrils flared.

"Sorry," I said, backing up. I watched Roy do his best to dodge those pesky red, pink and orange ghosts. He was playing better than his first attempt, but he was still no match to my talent.

"So what do you do for a living?" I asked. Roy needed to lower his stress level. He gripped the controller so tightly that the veins in his hands pulsed.

"I live," he finally answered.

"Excuse me?"

"I let the day dictate itself. I don't believe in being tied down to a job. It stifles my creative juices."

"What exactly do you need your creative juices for?"

"Everything," he grunted.

This man refused to give me a straight answer, which could only mean one thing. He was a bum and he somehow mooched enough money from some desperate soul so he could come and play video games on Tuesdays and Thursdays. It was probably an unsuspecting woman somewhere who was financing this date. I was disgusted.

"Maybe you can get a job here. I'm sure you can determine your own hours and they probably offer you a certain amount of credits to test the video games," I suggested.

Obviously health insurance and vested retirement funds weren't at the top of everyone's list. At this point, I was about helping Roy get gainfully employed. I'd always believed that you crossed paths with people for a reason. Maybe that was my purpose for meeting Roy.

"There's probably a way you can apply online," I said, continuing with my career counseling.

Roy shushed me and stopped me in the middle of the life coach spiel I was giving him. "You're messing up my flow," he growled.

No, he didn't.

I leaned against the Tetris game that was beside Ms. Pac-Man and entertained myself by counting the number of times that Roy tried to crush my top score. While he tried unsuccessfully to knock me out of the high rankings, I checked and answered emails, reviewed my online bank account statement, and researched cities within driving distance that I might want to venture to for my birthday.

The freckle-faced, red head girl happened to walk by and decided to look over Roy's shoulder. "You guys have been at this for a while. Are you having some kind of competition?"

"Something like that," I said.

"Who's winning?" She asked, running her teeth across her top retainer.

"Me," I boasted.

Roy scoffed. "It's on old game. I specialize in the updated stuff." He lifted his pants higher on his waist. "You know the things that were actually designed and manufactured in the twenty-first century."

The freckled-girl raised her pale hand to give me another high-five. "We know who runs the world."

Roy rolled his eyes at the sign of our female unity.

"I'm sick of this thing," he said, as a red ghost

gobbled up his last Ms. Pac-Man. "I'm going to play the games for real men."

Did he really say that? The games for real men?

Roy started a fast gait towards the front of the arcade and by the time I rounded the corner, he jumped on the simulated jet-ski racing game. I calmly slid my card and the machine deducted three credits. This was an expensive habit.

"Count down, baby," he said, standing up and leaning forward as the machine reared for action. From the time the green simulated flag flashed on the screen, Roy dipped, swerved and leaned his body in an effort to keep up with me. He rode my tail and tried to force my virtual jet ski into the bobbing barricades. Roy had no idea that while he only simulated the action, Trace had taught me how to ride and maneuver jet skis during one of our summer ventures to Lake Lanier last year.

Roy came in second.

"I need more credits on my card," I said.

"There's a machine up front and another one back near the bathrooms," Roy directed. He started another game without me and since he was clearly too peeved to finance this date, I decided to really unleash my competitive side. I liked to win—high school debate team, Scrabble, Taboo, cross country and not to mention one of the top twenty-five Atlanta brokers under the age of 40. Roy was the one who wasn't ready for the challenge. I never made it a point to crush a man's confidence since they always needed an extra stroke to their ego, but Roy had it coming to him.

"That was a lucky win," he told me. "This game takes hips. Men don't have hips.....I gave that one to you."

His excuses didn't stop. After thirty minutes, Roy finally bowed out, although not gracefully. I'd spent way too much money proving that my skills weren't a fluke. He was a chauvinistic pig and I'd wanted to break him down. I was out about fifty dollars because of it. It was time for me to leave and do something more productive with my day, but Roy happened to announce his intentions first.

"It's time for me to bounce," Roy said. He dug into all his pockets, producing a handful of arcade tickets every time. I pretended not to notice, but I knew he was looking for money.

"It was fun," I admitted. "Sometimes it's good to feel like a kid again."

No response. I hadn't expected one.

Roy yanked a fleece windbreaker and a baseball cap out of his backpack, and in twenty seconds made himself look like a teenager. I was sure he had potential, a talent of some sort, but he had no idea how to find it. I hoped he discovered it soon, though. There was more to life than getting your name on the top scorer board of a video game. But I couldn't change a man in one afternoon, and I knew from experience that you can't make a man what he doesn't want to be. I had my own issues to deal with, as my mom had so aptly reminded me.

"Do you need anything?"

"Anything like what?" he said. "Your career advice. Your sympathy? Your handouts?"

"Excuse me?"

"I see you with your expensive clothes. I saw you roll up in your ride. I'm not your type of dude. That's cool. A man at the barber shop hooked me up with the Mix and Mingle tickets. I was trying to find me a woman who I could flow with, but all I keep hooking up with are women like you."

I was wearing jeans, sneakers and an Atlanta Braves t-shirt that Bellamy had bought me from the game. What was so expensive looking about that? And I drove here in a car. So what? I worked hard. I'd been blessed and I wasn't going to apologize for it. I did have one question though.

"Women like me? And exactly what kind of woman would that be?"

"I know your type. From the jump, you walked in here thinking you were better than me."

I wasn't going to dignify Roy's foolishness with a response. Some things are better left unsaid. It was beginning to rain outside and it was close to rush hour. That was a bad combination.

"Be blessed," I said.

Roy mumbled something in response but I didn't care to hear another word from his mouth. If I knew how to contact the organizers of the Mix and Mingle event, I'd advise them to think twice about throwing in a twist. If I had struck up a conversation with a man like Roy at the event, I would've politely excused myself and saved both of us the time.

A whip of wind and then a pattering of raindrops drove into my face as I ran to the car. I used the Bluetooth system in the car to call Trace's office and got his voice mail.

"You've reached the office of Trace Moseley. I will be out of the office for the rest of the week, but checking voicemails periodically. If you need immediate assistance..."

I disconnected. Funny. He hadn't mentioned being out of the office last night.

I tried his cell phone and while it rang, I searched for an old receipt or piece of paper I

could use to jot down a grocery store list. No more baking. I needed real food. Salmon, yellow rice, and cabbage sounded like an easy and fulfilling option.

Trace answered the phone sounding out of breath.

"What in the world are you doing?"

"I was stuffing bags in the trunk," he said. "I tried to beat the rain, but it started pouring before I made it to the end of the parking lot."

"Call me back," I said. I noticed Roy walking out of the arcade. He was drenched like a mad cat.

"No, I'm good," Trace said. "What are you up to?"

I could hear the sound of a man's voice in the background and knew that Trace was listening to some kind of business book on audio. He listened to at least two books a month during his commute. After a moment, the background noise in his car stopped.

"I'm leaving the arcade," I said. "Don't even ask."

"I won't. I'll read about it."

I pulled out of the empty parking lot and headed towards the exit. Roy had walked up the street and was standing at the bus stop. He made a sad attempt to shield himself with his backpack, but it only made the rain puddle above his head.

"I called your office," I said. "I didn't know you'd taken off time from work. You didn't say anything about it."

"I hadn't planned on it," Trace said. "I'd put in for the time off a couple of months ago but wasn't sure if I was going to take it until last night. I was thinking about heading down to Fort Lauderdale to see my folks, but I haven't made up my mind yet."

I loved visiting Fort Lauderdale, but there was no way I'd ask to ride along. I'd made the trip with Trace twice to visit the Moseleys and each time left me pining for more sand and sun in my life. We'd lazily floated across the canals while we had a picnic dinner, and Trace and I were still able to take the short twenty-or-so mile ride to reach Miami and enjoy the nightlife.

"Your mom would love to have her prized possession

home for a few days," I said, even though I didn't want him to cross the Georgia line. "She'll probably run an announcement in the newspaper. She wants the world to know when her son is in town. The world and everybody else."

"Don't even say it," Trace said.

Although my mother had immediately fallen in love with Trace, it had taken some time for Mrs. Moseley to warm up to me. Her mind was settled on having Trace's high school and college sweetheart, Victoria, as her daughter-in-law. Trace and Victoria. They sounded like a couple on a soap opera.

"When are you leaving?"

"If I go, I'll head out Thursday morning."

"So what are you up to for the rest of the evening?" I asked. I merged into the mounting traffic on Interstate 85, heading south. I needed to detox myself from my outing with Roy.

"I'm going home to wrap gifts."

"Gifts? What's the occasion?" I asked, trying to squeeze in front of a woman driving a mini Cooper who didn't want to let me over. She put her window down and gave me the middle finger.

"I'm taking them to the shelter. I'm in one of my moods."

One of his giving moods, Trace meant. For as long as I'd known him, Trace had taken it upon himself to adopt one of the women's and children's shelters downtown. It wasn't part of his volunteer service for his job, or connected to his service at church. Trace did it purely from the goodness of his heart. The thing I loved about it was that Trace didn't wait for the typical times of the year like Christmas and Easter to visit the shelter, so the unexpected blessings were met with even more enthusiasm from the residents.

"And you're wrapping gifts? That's a first."

"I thought I'd try and do something different and wrap them instead of dropping them off in big plastic bags. Stephanie suggested it."

"Is she going to help you wrap them?" I asked.

Silence. I didn't like his silence.

"No," Trace said after a hesitation that lasted too long.

"I'll see how it goes. I may have gotten carried away. It seemed like a good idea when I was in the store."

"It's for a good cause," I said. "You'll get it done."

"Eventually. But it'll be quicker and easier if you help me."

Now I was the one who hesitated. I'd survived not getting sucked into the emotions of Christmas, New Year's and Valentine's Day without a man—without Trace. But I could slowly feel us inserting ourselves back into each other's lives. We were changing lanes again— from friends to more than friends. From my homey to my honey. Something about it felt natural, but I was cautious. The thought of falling in love and *staying* in love for a lifetime was overwhelming.

"Did you hear me?" Trace asked.

I didn't answer too quickly. Trace's home was comfortable and family-ready. Unlike many bachelors who barely owned enough furniture to fill two rooms, nearly every room in Trace's five-bedroom, three-and-a-half house was furnished, with help—he'd admitted—from his mother's discriminating eye. They'd taken care in choosing pieces to Trace's liking and personality. He'd chosen muted tones as the base color for the couches—browns, tans, and ivory. But he'd accentuated with colorful rugs, throw pillows and his growing art collection of pieces painted by local African-American artists. Trace had visited South Africa twice in the last eight years and had used pieces from Cape Town and Johannesburg for inspiration throughout the home. The back patio looked out upon a lake, and we'd watched many sunsets cuddled together in his free-standing hammock. Our love had grown there.

"I was planning on going home."

"We haven't hung out at my house in a long time," he rebutted.

"Trace –" I started.

"What are you scared of? I don't bite. Not that hard, anyway. When's the last time you've been over?"

I knew exactly when. It had been nine months ago on the Fourth of July. Kiysha and I stopped in for dinner before we headed to Lenox Square Mall for the fireworks display. Trace had wooed us over with the promise of beef ribs smothered in his special secret sauce, grilled corn on the cob, homemade slaw and baked beans. It was the three of us, even though I could tell that night that Trace wanted it to be us two. When Kiysha left to answer a private call, we were left together under a blanket of stars.

"You should've said yes. We would be planning a wedding right now," he'd told me. At the time, only three weeks had passed since I'd turned down his proposal. The pain was still evident in his eyes, but buried behind his deep brown eyes was also hope.

"I can't Trace. It's hard to explain. It's not that you're not a wonderful man."

"Then why?" he said, cupping my chin, turning my face towards him and saying words that still echoed within me. "Give me a reason."

Chapter 10

Trace opened his two-car garage so I wouldn't have to unload my groceries in the rain. He met me at the door leading into the kitchen and unhooked the plastic bag handles that were twisted around my fingers. I walked into his house and as always my eyes were drawn upward by the high vaulted ceilings. The architecture was undeniably stunning and I could tell by the sparkling countertops and stainless steel in the kitchen that housekeeping had been there today. The company he'd chosen used non-toxic, biodegradable cleaning supplies, but used a special natural lemony fragrance to mist the air.

I'd decided to cook my meal at Trace's house instead of waiting until I returned home. He had gadgets that even I didn't own. His mother had insisted he have handy gadgets to make cooking at home more convenient and less time consuming. The truth was, she liked having them when she visited. Trace rarely cooked, and when he did, he preferred throwing meat and veggies on his grill.

"When you said you'd gone shopping, I didn't think you'd cleared out the entire store." I followed the trails of shopping bags that ran along the back of his sectional couches. He had high ambitions for wanting to wrap everything. Even if he didn't run out of desire, he'd probably run out of wrapping paper.

I peeked in the bags by my feet. Barbies. Remote control cars. Play-Doh. Wrestling action figures. "Did you leave anything?"

"Some dust," Trace laughed. "When I think about coming home to an empty house with all of these bedrooms and no one to fill them, I realize how blessed I am. There are children sleeping three to a bed. There are families without beds at all who have to pack up the few belongings they have and lock them up so they'll still be there when they return at the end of the day. Will these toys take away the pain? No. But it never hurts to know somebody is thinking about you. Somebody cares."

Trace had a home of this magnitude because he'd purchased it with his future in mind. I knew he longed for the patter of little feet across the hardwood floors early in the mornings. He wanted to cook pancakes with silly faces made of out strawberries and whip cream. He was making a successful climb up his corporate ladder, and was now ready to trade in working long weekends for backyard barbecues with other couples. He knew the honeymoon phase of marriage didn't last forever, but he was up for the challenge. There would be arguments, but there would be the chance to kiss and make up. Trace wanted what I was scared to have.

Trace opened a bag filled with board games and Go-Fish card sets, then set it back in its place. He continued to rifle through bags until he found one with a princess tiara and wand set. He snapped the plastic tags that held the tiara in place and shook it to fluff the fake pink feathers glued around it. A single pink waft floated to the floor. I watched it, bowed my head slightly, and felt Trace set the tiara on my hair. He reached in the bag for a glittery wand and tapped it on my head before handing it to me.

I circled it through the air. "So you've crowned me a princess."

"Queen of my castle," Trace said.

I took off the tiara and placed it on the coffee table along with the wand. "Why do you say things like that?"

"Because I know what I feel and I can't always fight to keep the feelings I have for you inside. I don't see how you fight it. But even though you do, I see it in your eyes."

My gaze left him.

I walked back into the kitchen and Trace followed slowly behind me. His hands were stuffed into his back pockets.

"You say over and over how we're better as friends. But friends can grow to be lovers," he said. "Lovers for life."

I opened the cabinet that held a turntable of spices and seasonings. "Are you about to quote an old R&B ballad?" I asked light-heartedly. "Because that move is played out."

When I stood and turned around, Trace was an arm's length away from me.

"I don't need to use another man's words when I know what my heart is saying," Trace said.

"Your heart talks to you a lot when it comes to me," I said to him.

"All the time."

"Yet you risked losing me. It doesn't make sense."

"You know what they say. If you love something enough, let it go…" Trace's voice trailed off.

"I'm seeing the Mix and Mingle dates until the end. I have nothing to lose," I said, even though I wasn't so sure. This could be the day that Trace decided to move on. He certainly wasn't obligated to wait for me. He could toss and turn in his king-sized bed and wake up with a new resolution to move on without hopes of a future with Vaughn Holiday. There was still Stephanie. He didn't mention her and I'd learned from my first line of questioning not to ask. But I knew she was there.

And her call reminded me. Trace's phone buzzed across the counter. My eyes were quick and noticed

Stephanie's name before he picked it up.

"Excuse me for a minute," he said, disappearing down the long hallway towards his home office.

The tables had already turned. Trace had never taken a call out of the room when we were together. It made me think he had something to hide and there was more to his dates with Stephanie than he'd previously confessed. Who was to say their first date was actually their first?

The rain picked up from a sprinkle to a downpour. Drops pelted the kitchen bay window and traveled down the panes like tears.

Unexpectedly, my eyes begin to water. Tears pooled in the corners and I used the back of my hand to pat them away. Five minutes passed and Trace hadn't returned. Then ten minutes. When fifteen minutes had ticked away on his microwave clock, he reappeared.

"Ready to wrap? Or do you want to cook your food first?" he asked. He pushed back his floor to ceiling draperies in the adjoining living room.

"It doesn't matter," I said, immediately noticing the irritated tone in my voice.

"Are you okay?"

"I'm fine."

"Sure?" Trace looked at me with concern.

"Yes." Frustration crept through my body as I plopped down on the love seat across from him. There was more than enough space for us to work side by side, but I needed the space between us. We worked in silence until I was courageous enough to speak the words in my mind.

"You said it never hurts to know someone is thinking about you, and that someone cares," I said.

Trace pressed a piece of tape on a wrapping paper fold. He turned the box on its end.

"That's what I said," he said.

"I think about you. And I care." The confession breathed life back into me.

Chapter 11

I'd spent more time in bed than out of bed over the last two days, even to the point of eating my meals in bed. And I didn't feel the least bit guilty about it. Between chick flicks, action movies, and comedies on the movie channels that I never took the time to watch, I responded to comments on my blog. Numerous women claimed that the man who'd I'd called "Reese," aka Roy, was probably their sorry boyfriend or their no-good live-in adult son. Most of my comments were from women who wanted me to send their personal contact information to Huggy Bear. They were willing to offer their ovaries and womb to give him a baby, but I knew it was all a ploy to secure financial stability.

I wiggled my chilly toes and yearned for a pair of fluffy socks from my basket. I'd wait. It was too far to walk. Instead, I turned over to my laptop to read my blog posts one last time before publishing them to this World

Wide Web that had become my audience. Yesterday evening, I'd begrudgingly pulled myself out of bed for Mix and Mingle dates number seven and eight.

The first person I'd thought about calling was Trace but I'd already put too much on the line with him. After wrapping gifts for over an hour, I curled up in his love seat to catch a cat nap. When I awakened three hours later, the gloomy clouds had fallen lower in the sky, painting shades of misty greys and puffy white clouds across the horizon. He warmed up bowls of leftover chili for us to eat and it was the perfect end to the night.

My followers didn't know about my dilemma with Trace. How could I write about him when he was reading every word? Including these words...

DATES #6 and #7

Never tell yourself that it can't get any worse. It can. For the sake of anonymity, I'll call him Mr. Giggles.

Laughter is good for the soul. The Bible says something like that in Proverbs 17:22: A joyful heart is good medicine, but a crushed spirit dries up the bones. I know my blog posts may be intriguing, but they're nowhere near as insightful as the Holy Bible. And if you think that I have relationship problems, you should read about David and Bathsheba and Rachel and Leah. But anyway, back to Mr. Giggles. I didn't last an hour in the coffee shop with him. He reenacted his family Christmas memories that weren't funny in the least bit and giggled the entire time. Not laughed, giggled. Not chuckled, giggled. He reminded me of a Tickle-me Elmo that I'd bought for one of my baby cousins years ago.

The first time I experienced his high pitched squeal I thought it was part of his reenactment. Wrong. The joke was on me.

"I don't feel well," I told him once I'd had enough of people staring in my direction. "There's something going around my office."

Not long after, he excused himself to the restroom and returned smelling like he'd bathed in the awful, chemically smelling soap that they used in public restrooms. Obviously Mr. Giggles was also a germaphobe. Before we parted ways, he lifted his elbow so we could 'bump' our limbs instead of shaking hands or lean in for the casual hug that first dates usually give each other. He basically ran in the opposite direction and this time I was the one with the giggles.

But with Alston, my date to follow, nothing was funny.

I felt at ease when I walked into the quaint, artsy work space. I'd participated in one of these sip and stroke events before with my cousin in celebration of her birthday. We'd started with a blank canvas and ended with an abstract painting that I incorporated into my kitchen décor. Tonight's artistic piece was a surprise.

I was waiting in the back of the room, posted on one of the many wooden stools. Alston strode into the building with a single white rose and a bottle of red wine. Women turned. They swooned. They were envious. Had I been a spectator and not the recipient of this romantic show, I would've done the same. Imagine my surprise when he walked to the front of the room to begin the class.

Alston was engaging from the beginning, and he set our night on the right track when he introduced me as his date. He gave a brief overview of how to hold the paintbrush to achieve the desired brush strokes. He paid special attention to my technique and lingered near my work area to dish out painting advice and compliments.

"Impressive," Alston said, once I'd finished my painting of a woman lounging in the sunset. "This painting deserves to be on display."

"Flattery and exaggeration are two different things," I told him. "But thank you for the compliment."

"Then flatter me and let me take you to see my work," he said, lifting my hands into his. "My work is on exhibit about a block from here."

I agreed. Finally. A man with some class, right?

While me and the rest of the room were busy perfecting our paint stroke, Alston must've been taking some extra sips from the champagne glasses. The peppermint tucked in the corner of his jaw only slightly covered his breath that reeked of alcohol. Perhaps I was hypnotized by his charisma.

We arrived at the art gallery and through the window I could see the slightest shadow of a pallet on the floor, beside *it another bottle of wine. Atop it, a sprinkling of rose petals.*

Meta Holiday didn't raise a fool. I wasn't sure what kind of private showing Alston had expected, but he certainly wasn't going to get it from me.

I clicked the tab to publish my post for the awaiting three-thousand eight hundred and ninety seven subscribers. I was still amazed.

"Are you sure you don't want to come with me?" Kiysha said, bursting into my room. She'd stopped by to change into comfortable clothes before jumping on the road for a weekend road trip to Hilton Head, South Carolina. If the getaway had been strictly for pleasure, she wouldn't have complained. But since it was a work retreat, Kiysha knew the days before her held team building exercises and brainstorming sessions.

"I have a room all to myself and if you don't come I'll be forced to entertain Susan, and Susan works my last nerve." Kiysha propped her hands on her hips.

"I'm positive," I said, raising my arms above my head and pushing the stretch down through my toes. "I'm exactly where I want to be for now. I'll be fine."

"I'm starting to worry about you. You haven't been talking about houses, or contracts, or clients, or any of that. It's not like you."

"I've done enough to keep everybody happy," I said. "That's the point of taking a break for myself. It's all about *me.*"

Kiysha clasped her hands together and pretended to go down on one knee—but she didn't make it all the way down to the floor. "I'm *begging*. Have you *ever* in your *life* seen me beg before?"

I tapped a finger to my temple. "As a matter of fact, I haven't. I could use this to my advantage, you know."

"Come on. If you can go on all those disastrous dates with men you don't know, then you can ride with your favorite cousin to the beach. Think about it. I'll be holed up inside for most of the sessions anyway, but you can soak up some rays to bronze that beautiful brown skin of yours. And the waters. There's nothing like watching the endless ocean rippling across the horizon," she said dramatically."

"Keep going." I propped my hands behind my head.

"You can meditate on some scripture, think about God's goodness, and dream about your fabulous future with Trace."

I never should've mentioned to Kiysha that I'd gone to Trace's house. That only fueled her hope that the three carat ring stored in his home office safe would soon find its home on my finger."

"You can't let it go."

"I will never let it go." Kiysha snatched the covers off my legs, leaving my bottom half completely exposed. I'd always hated wearing pajamas bottoms.

"You're nasty," Kiysha said, throwing the covers back in a clump on top of me. "That's why you need a husband."

133

"I'm in my house and my bed."

"You should see the beds at this resort," Kiysha boasted, returning to her mission. "They're huge, pillow-top mattresses that are more comfortable than the clouds in heaven." Kiysha swept her arms skyward.

"You almost had me until that part," I joked. "I can't stand sleeping on strange sheets and under the covers where people have done who knows what with who knows who." I scrunched my face up at the thought of it. "No, thank you."

"One day you're going to need me," Kiysha said.

"Thank God it's not today. Good-bye."

Kiysha left, but not before disappearing into my bathroom and scrounging through my toiletries to find a tube of sunblock and a half-empty bottle of insect repellant.

"Have fun," I yelled after her. "Call me when you get there."

"I'm not talking to you anymore. Ever."

"Lies."

"Sooner or later you're going to have to get up and wash your booty before you go on that date tonight. What's the crazy man's name this time?"

"Why does he have to be crazy?"

"Based on your track record it should be an adventurous night."

"Wait a minute. I thought you weren't supposed to be talking to me anymore." There was no response. "Hello?"

Kiysha was meddling in the kitchen. I could hear her opening and closing the cabinet doors so I knew she was now on a hunt for traveling snacks and drinks. She was in luck. I'd stocked up on my trip to the grocery store with all of the foods we loved to munch on during movie night and our impromptu sleepovers. I'd even bought two bags of her favorite trail mix with the M&Ms and hidden them behind the aluminum foil. I would tell her. But she wasn't talking to me.

Kiysha left without a word. As her mother always said, "She's a piece of work."

But she was right. I needed to get moving if wanted to be on time for my outing tonight with Michael, or the next so called "crazy" as Kiysha deemed him.

To their delight, my latest clients had won the bidding war for the house they wanted, which meant in the next thirty days or so, I'd have a sizable commission check. Which also meant I could splurge on my birthday getaway in two weeks and not have to worry about blowing a little money.

I'd allotted myself two hours to handle my pending real estate requests, emails from my broker's office, and questions from my clients. By six o'clock, I was headed towards downtown to meet Michael at Sky View, the latest Ferris Wheel attraction that had come to Atlanta. I'd seen all the latest features on the local morning shows when it had first opened, but I'd yet to have the chance to experience it, though Trace had mentioned taking the ride several times.

Like most cities in America, Atlanta had its share of budget cuts, city council fights over finances and in my opinion misguided funds. There were other things I could've suggested they do with their money besides constructing a Ferris wheel near the Centennial Olympic Park. The area was already congested, but Atlanta did what it needed to do to keep Georgians coming into downtown and visitors streaming into the city.

I parked at a nearby Park-And-Ride lot and found Michael waiting for me at the attendant's booth like he'd promised.

"Vaughn? I'm Michael."

"Hi, Michael." His voice was incredible. Late night, quiet storm on the radio, make a girl do things she shouldn't kind of incredible.

"Your voice is amazing. I'm sure people tell you that all the time." We shook hands.

"Thanks. They do," he admitted. "But it's always nice to hear it from a beautiful woman."

Michael was handsome, too, but that was never something I'd tell a man the first time I saw him. I always believed the good-looking ones knew when they could grab a woman's attention. Not necessarily cocky, but confident.

"Have you been on this Ferris wheel before?" I asked. I shielded my eyes and looked up to the top. The website said it was two-hundred feet in the air.

"I haven't been on it yet. I heard it gives a great view of the city."

"I bet it's going to be breathtaking," I agreed. "Let's see what all of the hoopla is about."

"Ladies, first."

Michael paid the attendant and we stepped into the gondola. We settled into the seat and our pod moved slightly as the couple who'd walked up in line behind us were loaded into their gondola.

"Is it hot in here to you?" Michael asked. He swept his palm across his forehead.

"Feels fine to me," I said. "You aren't claustrophobic, are you?"

"Not at all," he said, turning his entire body towards me. "So tell me about yourself. What do you like to do? What's your profession?"

"I like cupcakes and real estate," I said. "Which is why I love to bake and sell high quality homes."

Michael nodded. He glanced out of the gondola when we slightly moved again. He turned back towards me and wiped his hands across the knees of his jeans. "So forget the homes. I'm more interested in the cupcakes. What's your specialty?"

"Anything your sweet tooth wants," I bragged.

"Is that an offer?" he asked.

"Only if you're a paying customer."

He laughed, I laughed. But I was serious. Vaughn's Delights was for business, not for handouts.

Our gondola moved and the Ferris wheel started its slow ascent. "We're on our way up," I announced.

I settled back against the seat so I could take in the Atlanta skyline. It wasn't like I hadn't seen the CNN Center, the Georgia Dome, or the Equifax building before, but going higher gave me a new perspective. Atlanta was a beautiful city.

"Oh, look over there," I said, pointing in the direction of the water fountains at Centennial Olympic Park. "They're starting that water show that's synchronized with the music."

Michael didn't answer. He'd leaned forward with his elbows propped on his knees and his face resting in his palms.

"Are you alright?" I said. I leaned forward to get a better view of his face, but he'd shielded his expression from me.

"This isn't good." Michael's muffled voice squeaked.

Where was the bass in his voice? Where was the voice that made women like me swoon?

I studied the top of the gondola for the blinking, pin-sized, red light of the hidden camera because surely this couldn't be another disaster.

I rolled my eyes. "What's wrong?" I said, knowing my voice held little, if any, compassion.

"I'm having a hard time breathing," Michael said.

"I thought you said you weren't claustrophobic."

"I'm not. But I think I might be scared of heights now."

"You think? How does a person *think* they're scared of heights? Either you are or you aren't. We're two-hundred feet in the air and you don't know whether you're scared of heights? "Unbelievable," I muttered.

"My last plane ride. A storm. The turbulence." Michael was almost panting. "I thought we were going down." He wiped his brow. "I need a paper bag. Something to breathe in. Maybe that will help."

What would help is if Michael hadn't invited me to view the city in this thing in the first place. And who carries a paper bag in their purse? The only thing I had worth looking for was my Taser. Maybe I could jolt him and temporarily put him out of his misery until both of his feet were safely on the ground.

I laughed. I laughed like I'd done on that ridiculous date with Carl.

"What's so funny?"

I tried to stifle my outburst but the more I tried, the funnier it seemed. When I finally got a hold of myself I asked, "Did you seriously ask me that question?"

He squeaked. Again.

Lord, what are you trying to show me? Because I need the answer. So these blind dates were a bad idea? I get it. I'm done.

"Try opening your eyes," I said. "It's really not that bad."

"No. I'm good."

"I can see a very clear view of Centennial Olympic

Park. Did you live here during the Olympics?"

No response.

"Michael?" I prayed this man hadn't gone off and died. I could see the headlines now. Young Atlanta Power Real Estate Agent Under Investigation For Murder. "Michael? Please answer so I know you're alright."

"I'm fine," he muttered. "I'm ready to get off of this thing." He uttered curse words under his breath.

I fished a peppermint from my purse and pushed it into the open space between his sweaty fingers. "A peppermint. Maybe that will help."

"Get me down. That will help."

I stopped and thought about the situation and how horribly embarrassed Michael must've felt. There wasn't a man I knew who would put himself in a situation to be humiliated in front of a woman he didn't know. If the shoe were on the other foot, I'd expect my date to show some kindness. Poor fellow. I felt bad about his predicament, but worse about how rude I'd been towards him.

I tentatively placed a hand on his shoulder. "We can't get out right now, but it will be over before you know it. I promise. Keep your eyes closed and focus on something else."

"I'm sorry about this," he said. His breathing seemed to have slowed down to a calmer pace.

"Don't worry about it. How was your day?"

"Not bad," Michael answered, then began to bore me by talking about his job as a development officer at one of the smaller local colleges. As long as he was talking, breathing, and distracted, I'd endure his stories.

My phone chirped, signaling a text message. It was Trace. He'd decided to use his vacation time later and put off going to Fort Lauderdale.

Having fun?

No. Read blog 2nite.

Want company?

Sure. Bring wings.

U eat a lot.

U do too.

U use me.

U love it.

Nearly ten minutes later, we'd completed the entire rotation and the only view now was the parking lot below our feet.

"You made it," I said, patting him on the back.

He peeked from between his fingers and said, "Thank you, Jesus."

He took the words right out of my mouth.

Michael jumped out of the gondola before I had a chance to stand up. At least he was chivalrous and held his hand out to help me step down.

"I've already made a fool out of myself," he said to me, though he wouldn't look directly

at me. "Would I be more of a fool if I asked you if we

could still have dinner and drinks?

I would come off as an idiot if I said 'no' to his request, but I had to look at this experience realistically. I loved to travel to places that couldn't be reached by car. Michael couldn't endure a ten-minute rotation on a Ferris wheel so I doubted very seriously after his traumatic experience that he'd board another plane. We would never work. We'd be miserable together. I couldn't be swayed by what I thought his opinion would be of me. He didn't even know my last name, and three weeks from now, he probably wouldn't even remember my first.

"The Park Bar is down the street," Michael said, hopeful.

I must've taken too long to answer because he rightly assumed my answer was no.

"Don't worry about it. Your silence has said enough," he said with a crooked smile. He pounded his chest with his fist. "I'm a man. I can take it."

"I wouldn't think twice about it. Everybody is scared of something. I'm terrified of spiders."

"Oh, so if I'd rescued you from a granddaddy long legs spider then I'd be your dream date."

"Exactly," I said.

"Next time?"

"Next time," I said, even though we both knew there wouldn't be a next time.

Michael held his arms open. "Can I at least get a hug?"

"Sure," I said.

He folded me into his broad chest and embraced me like I was his woman. There was nothing like a strong squeeze with biceps and triceps attached. I'd always loved a great hug from a man. When we pulled away from each other, the Skyview attendant was staring us down.

"Nice ride wasn't it? Got you all hot and bothered. I can tell. You should go home and finish the night off right."

I had this way of saying things with my eyes that could quickly shut a conversation down. I'd perfected it after years of watching my mother, since she could produce one of those looks at lightning speed. I gave one of those looks to the attendant. Some people have no home training.

"Sir, our night is already finished," Michael said. He looked at his watch. "All fifteen minutes of it."

He walked me back to my car, strolling slowly like he didn't want the evening to end.

I beeped the alarm on my car as we approached.

He whistled. "You must make a hell of a lot of money selling those houses and cupcakes. Do you have a card on you?"

"I sure don't." I lied. I always had my business contact information because I never knew when I'd come across the opportunity to service a new client. However, Michael never was and never would be one of my clients.

"I'll be in the market for a house soon. What's your last name? I'll look you up."

I knew he would. And he would become a pest. I could tell by the way he was clinging around the car.

"You have my email," I told him. "Trust me. That's the quickest way to get in touch with me."

"Then look for an email from me soon. I like a challenge. You might be thinking about me in a certain way, but there's more man to me that you didn't see. I might be scared of heights, but I'm not scared of love."

I cleared my throat, not sure how to answer. "Nice to meet you, Michael," I said. "I've got to get doing."

Before I had a chance to react, he lifted my hand and kissed it. I wanted to check for blood. They were the roughest lips I'd ever felt. Nothing like Trace's. Michael should stick to hugging.

"Until next time," he said, dropping his baritone voice even lower. That didn't do a thing for me. I'd already heard him scream like Michael Jackson so the thrill was gone.

And I was gone, too.

"Call Trace," I spoke to my bluetooth when I was finally pulling out on Luckie Street. "Hey, I'm on my way home."

"Change of plans," Trace said. "We're going out. I'm running by home to change, but I'll be there as soon as I can."

"Where are we going?"

"Do you have to know everything?"

"Preferably. You act like you don't know that about me."

"I know more about you than you realize," Trace said.

My stomach had butterflies because I knew what was happening. Love was having its way and I no longer wanted to fight it.

Chapter 12

Childhood memories of going to the fair in Denver rushed into my head as soon as I stepped beyond the gate of the Atlanta Fair. Unfortunately one of those memories included Bryant, so I had to push that dreadful kissing mistake out of my head, but other than that I was about to be a kid again. I guess with the whole video arcade debacle something had gotten into me.

"This is the last week that the fair is going to be here," Trace said as he bought two armbands for unlimited rides. "Every year I say I'm coming or that I'm going to bring one of the boys I mentor, but I never get around to it."

"So who did you really want to come for? Me or you?"

"Me, of course. But a grown man can't exactly roam around a fair alone without getting strange looks," he confessed. "The last thing I need is to be followed by a police officer."

"Ain't that the truth," I said. I held out my wrist so he could attach the neon yellow band.

"This is better than wings and sitting in front of the television right? It never hurts to get out and have a little fun."

The Ferris wheel was positioned in the middle of the fair and towered over most of the attractions. A bright rainbow of oversized bulbs lit up the sides of the wheel and music pumped out of hidden speakers.

"Let's go on the Ferris Wheel first," I suggested even though it looked like it could use an extra inspection from an engineer. "I need to make up for tonight."

"Tell me about it."

"You'll have to read it on my blog," I said, smiling. "Did you know I have almost six-thousand subscribers now? I'm becoming pretty popular in the blogosphere these days."

"Your blog is popular. No one has any idea who you are."

"Ingenious idea, right? Anonymity makes it even more mysterious. And I have a career to uphold. I'm going places, doing big things. I can't be the face of Atlanta's dismal dating scene."

"And you shouldn't be."

There was no one waiting in line, but Trace and I still had to weave through the metal partitions to reach the area where we could board the Ferris wheel.

"All aboard lady and gent," the ticket taker said

when we reached the front. He tipped his hat and stretched his arms out from end to end. He gave the two of us a performance like the line for his attraction stretched through the fair grounds and circled the parking lot.

"You are about to step on the best ride this side of the Mason Dixon line. There's not another Ferris Wheel that can lift you on a smoother ride, glide you through the Atlanta sky, or light up your life. Last night a couple went up dating, and came back down engaged. This Ferris Wheel will take your love to the highest level."

"Then what am I waiting for?" Trace said, pulling my hand.

The ticket taker wiggled his bushy eyebrows, then bowed and swept his top hat in front of us as we passed.

"I've heard about people being excited about their jobs but I think he's a little over the top," I whispered.

"Our lives are in his hands," Trace whispered back. "You might want to keep your comments to yourself."

I jabbed him in the ribs with my elbow and we settled back into the space only big enough for two average-sized people or one oversized man.

The Ferris wheel operator tweaked the side of his handlebar mustache, reminding me of my tenth grade Chemistry teacher, Mr. Calhoun. He looked up towards the sky. "There's a full moon tonight. Strange things are bound to happen."

"Trust me. They've already started," I laughed.

The metal safety bar came down with a loud clank and I instinctively scooted as close as I could to Trace. I settled into the familiarity of his scent and he lifted his arm and put it around my shoulder.

"I wonder when this thing was inspected last."

I kicked a hardened piece of pink bubble gum into the corner. "Don't do it. Don't you go crazy on me. I've had enough for one night."

Trace thumbed the edge of his nose. "There's nothing but bravery in this heart. As long as you're with me, you don't have anything to worry about. There's a Superman cape under these clothes. I wouldn't let anything happen to you."

I believed him. God, I believed Trace. He was everything I'd ever prayed for, and some of what I hadn't. But what if I wasn't the woman he thought I was?

My major fear was hurting Trace because of my issues with commitment. Yes, I'd done that self-reflecting my mom had talked about it. I'd looked at myself in my bathroom mirror and said, *"You are scared of commitment. Your future is being held hostage by your past."*

An occasional creak of the wheel sang along with the carnival-themed music that filled the air. There was the slight scent of oil and rubber, but I could still smell the aroma of funnel cakes. Hot, powdered with white sugar, and drizzled with fudge on one half was how I liked mine.

Trace and I went an entire rotation before we spoke another word. Although we'd been spending a considerable amount of time together over the last few weeks, something about tonight felt different. I wanted him to sweep the hair away from my face and kiss me on my neck like he used to do. I wished that he would rub his hand on my forearm and let it settle in an unassuming way on my knee, to let me know that even when we weren't saying a word, I was on his mind.

It didn't surprise me when he said, "Give me a reason why we shouldn't be together?"

I let his question linger, because I felt like it was a trick question. I knew that no matter what answer I gave him, Trace would have a rebuttal. And he would be right. There was only one true reason. I was scared. Make that terrified. I'd given my all to a man before. I'd laid it all on the line before with nothing to show for it but broken dreams and promises.

"You can't say anything, because there isn't one," Trace said in my silence.

"I can come up with plenty," I said.

"But they wouldn't be true."

Then he did that thing. Brushed my hair away from the side of my face. But a kiss didn't follow.

"Maybe *you* should give *me* a reason why we *should* be together," I turned back on him. I'd given him back the words he'd given to me that Fourth of July night.

We'd circled around to the bottom of the ride again,

but Trace signaled to the game operator to take it up another time. The man eagerly obliged.

In the small space of the Ferris wheel cart Trace still managed to wrap his arms around me. "I don't have a problem expressing my feelings for you. You know that. You want one reason why we should be together, but I can give you thousands."

Then came the kiss. My feelings for Trace that I'd been trying to suppress bubbled over like a fountain. I was tired of running. I'd missed him.

Chapter 13

Now that she'd returned from her work retreat rejuvenated and having survived a weekend with her co-worker, Susan, Kiysha had volunteered to bring homemade desserts for their office potluck. This, of course, meant that I'd be doing the majority of the mixing and other preparations while she watched. I'd opened the door to find her holding two grocery bags filled with flour, sugar, butter, eggs, multiple boxed cake mixes, bagged candies, food coloring and frosting. When I told her that I'd dumped my commitment issues, her exact words were: "Hallelujah and thank you, Jesus. There is a God in heaven."

"So do you think I made the right decision?"

"Is that a trick question? You should've made this decision a long time ago. You better be thankful that Trace isn't the kind of man who'll run behind anything wearing panties that smiles at him. It's not like he has to beg women for attention."

"Are you finished?" I asked.

"No. Because I was going to be the one having to wipe away your tears when Trace moved on to another woman and left you wallowing in misery."

"I'm not one to wallow in misery."

"That's what they all say," Kiysha said, piping the bagged frosting into a perfect flower on top of one of the cupcakes. Last summer I'd forced her to take a cake decorating class with me and I was thrilled to see she hadn't lost her skills for perfect petals. On another day, Kiysha would've already been complaining about her easy contribution to this daunting task, but she'd been over-the-top happy since I told her that I and Trace were …trying again. A second chance for me.

"There's no guarantee that this is going to end up in a happily ever after," I said, trying not to get my expectations too high.

"Maybe not, but it's a guarantee that going out with Trace again is going to be a heck of a lot more stable than what you've encountered over the last two weeks."

"Did I tell you what he said?" I slid the oven mitt of my hand and gently pushed the middle of one of the cupcakes with my pinkie finger.

"What?" Kiysha egged me on. "I know it was romantic. Man, that Trace needs a clone."

"He said he's stepping in where the other men would've been. He's taking me on my last four Mix &

Mingle dates." I crossed my arms across my chest. "And he actually expects me to blog about it."

"And why not? You blogged about all the other foolishness," Kiysha said. "But at least now you can give these Atlanta women some hope. I'm here to tell you, other than Huggy Bear, you'd painted a grim picture for us single ladies. It was hilarious, but it was grim."

I snapped my fingers at the idea that had popped in my head.

"You're going to love me for this, Kiysha," I said.

"Vaughn Holiday, I know that look on your face and I don't like it one bit. The answer is no."

"You haven't heard what I have to say."

"And I don't have to." Kiysha dropped an empty piping bag into the garbage and picked up a full one.

"You should go out with the men on my last four Mix and Mingle dates. I've already coordinated the day and times so all you have to do is show up. It'll be fun."

"You call the dates you've been on fun? Girl, please." She covered her finished cupcake tray with a plastic container top, then sighed. "But I'll do it for you because the last thing I want to do is disappoint my favorite cousin. And besides, I have nothing else to do with my life right now anyway. I think God wanted you to weed out all of the crazies so you could get to the real deal. That's why I'm happy to oblige. You know the Lord does work in mysterious ways," she said, snapping her fingers. "So tell me about mystery men numbers nine, ten, eleven and twelve."

"I know absolutely nothing about them, except that you're going out with Dr. Govan Phillips."

"Govan? That name sounds like money. Carry on."

"He wanted to meet today at lunchtime at Rays on the River but I never did respond. It's still early. I'm going to email him and let him know that my beloved, talented, intelligent and fiercely sexy cousin is coming in my place."

"You do that," Kiysha said, doing a dramatic twirl. "And make sure you tell the good doctor to be ready for all this. In the meantime, I'll finish icing these cupcakes and you can get ready for your night with Trace. Where are you going?"

"He didn't say. You know how he is. My only instructions were to dress comfortably in jeans." I held up a finger. "And don't start trying to give me a lesson in fashion."

"I'm just saying. I know you stay cute and all, but don't get too complacent with Trace because he's an old flame. Keep the spark lit, sweetheart. You want him to fan the flames, not blow them out."

"I've got it covered." I'd already thought about what I wanted to wear. I'd searched my closet like this was our second date. Trace had already seen me in my ball gown best, my rattiest sweat pants worse, and all things in between. Still, that didn't stop me from agonizing over the perfect pair of jeans to accentuate my shape. Eventually, I sought Kiysha's opinion—which she was more than happy to give—and I finished getting ready. I slipped on my clothes, brushed my hair back into a ponytail at the nape of my neck, and put on my favorite pair of sterling silver hoop earrings. A good pair of earrings and the perfect shade of lipstick could make every woman look like an effortless beauty. For good measure, I brushed on a thick coat of extra black, lash lengthening mascara to make my eyes pop. A tip courtesy of the beauty section in Essence Magazine.

I returned to my living room to find Kiysha standing on my balcony swirling a glass of red wine. She looked at me from head to toe when I slid open the glass door.

"Good enough."

"You should be happy we're family, otherwise I would've fired you as my best friend a long time ago."

"Anything you wear is better than that horrible t-shirt you used to have with the huge GOD IS MY MAN mantra on the front. That was ridiculous. I'm glad you pulled yourself out of that rut."

"It's still true. God is my man," I said. I leaned against the top railing. "I have no idea where that shirt disappeared to. I thought I left it in Denver, but Mom never found it and Jazzy P promised me he hadn't shredded it to use to wax his car."

"Don't bother looking for the shirt," Kiysha said, sipping from her glass. "You'll never find it. Never." Kiysha pushed one of my patio chairs toward me with her big toe, her way to invite me to sit. "God *should* be your first love. He loved you so much that He blessed you with a man like Trace that truly loves you. Do I think Trace is perfect? Absolutely not. But who is?"

Kiysha stretched and lifted her legs so she could prop them on the top of the patio rail. "If you're looking for a man who's perfect, I'm afraid none of us will ever find him. But that man—right there—has found you. Keep your eyes and your heart open so you won't miss your blessing."

I followed Kiysha's gaze to the parking lot below us. Trace was pulling into an empty visitor's parking space. He stepped out of the car, never noticing that he was being watched.

"I told him to call me when he was almost here and I'd meet him downstairs," I said. "Why is he coming up?"

"Because he's a gentleman," Kiysha said.

Once Trace had disappeared from my view, I noticed the same couple in the parking lot who'd been tangled together two weeks ago when Trace brought over the Mix & Mingle tickets. Unlike last time when they couldn't keep their roaming lips and hands off of each other, they seemed to be embroiled in a heated argument. Her hands fought the air in frustration and he clenched the hair on both sides of his head as if the mere sound of her voice was giving him a migraine. That was love sometimes. Up one minute. Down the next. That was the last thing I needed to see.

"You know," Kiysha said. "You only made it through eight dates."

My breath caught.

"Don't act like you've had a bout of amnesia," she said.

I protested. "But I'm not going on the rest of the dates because of Trace. Isn't that what you've always wanted for me?"

Kiysha slid open the patio door and I followed her inside. "What's that got to do with our deal?"

"You wouldn't do this to me," I said, sliding on my shoes.

"Yes, I would."

Kiysha didn't sound serious, but because she wouldn't look me in the face, I couldn't tell what was truly going on in her mind. I needed to drum up some tears.

"I'll let the dollhouse stay here a few more days so you'll have the chance to say good-bye," she said, beginning to pack up her cupcakes, save for the one she was devouring.

"Fine," I said, saying anything to make her think I was in agreement. That dollhouse wasn't leaving. I didn't care if I'd only been on eight dates.

"Real talk." Kiysha said. She was balancing boxes of Vaughn's Delights in her arms.

"You are the fabulous Vaughn Holiday and you deserve every good thing that's coming to you. God's written a story specifically for you. Live in it. Enjoy it with all of its ups and downs and bends and curves, because God is in control."

Kiysha was always comical, but every now and then she showed her sentimental side. This girl was about to make me cry, for real this time.

"And isn't He much better at leading my life than I am?" I said.

"He is. Because I tell you if I read about another one of your pitiful dates I was going to report every last detail to your mother. She would've shut things down real quick."

"Quicker than quick."

"But she at least needs to know about your kissing cousin." Every time she brought the subject up, Kiysha frowned like she had a bad taste in her mouth.

"Eventually I *will* tell her about Bryant, *sans* the details," I said, walking to the door at the sound of the buzzer.

Knots turned over in my belly. Butterflies. All of sudden he'd given me butterflies. I'd know Trace for two years, dated him for one, and he'd asked for my hand in marriage. We'd loved each other and argued with each other. We'd even prayed together about important decisions in our lives. He wasn't a stranger. But when I opened the door, I saw Trace with new eyes.

"Hi," he said. The gleam in his eyes when he looked at me was evident. When he walked into my condo, we crossed back into familiar territory, and I nearly melted when he put his arms around me. God, I could stay here forever, I thought.

"Mmmmm. You smell good," I said. He pulled away and kissed me on the cheek. I wanted to tell him he'd missed the bullseye. My lips were waiting. However, since Kiysha was grinning from ear to ear in fascination while she watched us, I'd save those words for later.

"Why don't you two walk down the aisle today and forego all the wedding madness? Trace, call one of your minister friends and we can do it right now." She picked up the straggly piece of fake mistletoe that was still on my coffee table and pretended to hold it like a bouquet of flowers. "You've got your bridesmaid here."

"I'd do it in a minute," Trace said with no hesitation.

The silence hung between all three of us and their eyes fell on me.

"Stop playing. Let's go," I said to Trace. "As far as I'm concerned this is a relationship re-do. We are officially on our first date."

"Then I'm guilty of love at first sight."

Kiysha threw her hands in the air. "See, that's what I'm talking about. Trace, I need to have a serious talk with your parents and ask them why they only had one son."

Kiysha was inflating Trace's ego, but he was too humble to show it. "It's going to take a special man for you, Kiysha. Put in some extra prayers."

"Oh, I have been. And I'm hoping this Mix & Mingle date that your sweetie passed to me with Doctor Govan Phillips, is going to be the answer to those prayers."

Trace looked at me and I already knew what he was about to say.

"What's the harm? Because it didn't work out for me, doesn't mean it won't work out for Kiysha." I wrapped my hand around his arm and led him towards the door.

"Shouldn't we be leaving? We're leaving," I answered for him. "Kiysha, can you lock up for me?"

"No problem. I'll lock your door and *you* unlock your heart."

Kiysha winked at me. We both knew the same thing. That had already been done.

Chapter 14

My trekking around Atlanta and the surrounding area rarely took me too far east of the city, but I enjoyed visiting the less congested areas. The further we drove away from the city, the slower life became.

When Trace exited the highway, he still refused to answer my questions about our destination. It was another twenty minutes before we pulled into a graveled driveway. His car's tires crunched over the rocks on the long and winding driveway that led back to a set of horse stables, a picturesque view that took my breath away. Beyond the stable was a lake bordered by lush green trees. I closed my eyes and imagined this was what paradise looked like.

"So now you know what's going down," he said, following wood carved signs that directed cars to a parking area. There were only three other cars on the property.

"I assume we're riding horses, but knowing you, it could be something totally different from what I expect."

"I'm keeping it simple today," he said. "Besides, you've probably forgotten that you still owe me this date from over a year ago."

Despite what he thought, I hadn't forgotten. Trace and I had made plans to go horseback riding on the day I broke up with him. It had been a long and exhausting conversation with plenty of tears on my part. Confusion and disappointment on his part. He'd endured my rejection proposal, but he thought we were going to continue working on our relationship.

"I remember the day," I said, quietly. "It was a hard one."

Trace nodded but didn't speak, so I continued.

"What if I'm not the woman you expect me to be? What if after it's all said and done, I don't fit the ideal picture of what you want for your life?"

"And what if you do? But what if you don't want me? I could put myself out there and you could change your mind and walk away at any moment. But that's the chance I'm willing to take."

Our conversation was taking a shift to a serious tone, nothing like the lighthearted conversation we'd had on our way here. We could numerate the 'what if's' all day, but now wasn't the time for it.

"Let's not go there right now," I said.

Trace swept my hair away from my face in agreement,

then took his key out of the ignition. He came around to open my car door, and we walked hand-in-hand to the front opening of one of the stables.

"Ahhh. The smell of nature and fresh manure," I said.

"Farm living. That's why I'm a city boy. Give me asphalt and exhaust fumes any day."

The woman who appeared from behind the stable doors was wearing a hot pink t-shirt, dusty, broken-in jeans, and knee-high riding boots. Her hair was the same color as the hay that carpeted the stable floor and it was pulled back into a high ponytail that trailed the length of her back and down to her waistline.

"You must be Trace," she said with a slight Southern twang. "I'm Emma. Nice to finally meet you. I'm all set and ready to go if you are." She turned to me. "And your lovely guest is?"

"I'm Vaughn."

"Vaughn? What a unique name. Sounds like a celebrity."

"Thank you," I said, taking her outstretched hand. "But no paparazzi here." I expected her palms to feel rough and calloused but they were remarkably soft and a bit cool to the touch. A horse belted out an intimidating "neigh" that made me jump.

"I've wanted to go horseback riding since I was a teenager, but now that I'm here I'm scared out of my wits."

"Don't be," Emma said. "Our horses are trained and

very gentle. They are used to being ridden and they have a way of sensing riders who are uneasy, so they stay calm. You'll be comfortable and you'll enjoy yourself."

Emma's words did nothing to ease my anxiety. It only increased when a man wearing a cowboy hat led two horses out by the reins—one midnight black and the other the most perfect shade of brown I'd ever seen. Their nostrils flared open as the man held his hands out for them to eat some food from his palm. The brown horse seemed to pay close attention to me with his wide, almost black eyes. I wasn't sure if it was trying to connect with me, or picturing how he could eat me for dinner.

"I hope he doesn't like dark meat," I whispered to Trace.

Emma walked over to the brown horse. "This is Cocoa. I think she likes you. Come a little closer. She's harmless."

So who was this woman now? The horse whisperer? I took two tentative steps toward the horse. It blinked, but otherwise didn't move.

"Go ahead, Vaughn," Trace coaxed. "Feed her something."

I cut my eyes at him. "I actually like having my hand attached to my wrist," I said in a low voice so I wouldn't startle the horse. "You do it."

"No, I'm good," he said, shaking his head when the cowboy offered him a handful of grain. "I'll stick to riding."

"That's what I thought," I snickered.

After a brief riding lesson and instructions on handling the reins, Trace and I mounted the horses. The saddle was hard on my tush and I felt I was sitting higher than the horse actually looked. A few minutes passed before my clinched knees relaxed and my hands loosened their death grip on the leather reins. Before long, my entire body fell into a rhythm as we trotted down a woodsy path. Beyond the brush, I could still see the lake and two cabanas in the distance. Geese floated lazily across the water, bobbing their heads in and out in search of fish.

At a synchronized gait, Trace and I rode side by side and Emma was a few feet ahead of us.

"See what you missed last time?" Trace said.

"I've missed more than horseback riding all of this time," I said. Our eyes met. "I've missed you, too."

"I saw you almost twice a week for the most part."

"I know. But you know what I mean. I missed you. I missed us. I didn't really realize it until these last couple of days since we decided to go down this road of second chances. But then again, it's easy to see how great somebody is when you've had the kind of dates like I've had over the past couple of weeks."

"The cream always rises to the top," Trace said. "I rolled my dice with that move, but your knight in shining armor rode in on this horse today to save you."

"You're a mess."

"Then, clean me up, baby. Clean me up.

We rode on the trail for another twenty minute before Emma led us through an area

where the trees arched into a natural awning. I ducked to prevent the last section of brush from sweeping across my face. Led by their natural instinct, the horses headed towards the lake.

"I take it they need water," I said to Trace as they eased up on the water's edge.

"Or maybe you need wine," Trace said. He dismounted his horse and came over to help me. That's when I noticed a quilt spread out near the bank of the lake, approximately two hundred feet from where our horses had stopped to drink. Emma walked over to corral our two stallions.

We held hands again as walked through the thick carpet of grass. "I don't think you can help yourself. You've always got to put an extra touch on things to make them special."

"You don't get very far in life by doing the minimum," Trace said.

Emma and the horses had wandered to the far end of the lake. It was the perfect Saturday afternoon, and if there had been a cloud in the sky I would've been floating on it. Trace opened a brown wicker basket and unstrapped the bottle of wine inside.

"Reason number one....," he said, tipping the bottle to fill my glass halfway.

"Reason?"

"On the Ferris wheel you said you wanted to know a reason why we should be together, but I have more than one. So reason number one. I know that your favorite type of wine is pomegranate Kosher wine, slightly chilled. Number two. I've watched how you love to eat pecans, but then you always complain that they irritate the roof of your mouth. Number three. I love the way your little pinkie toenail on your left foot grows a little crooked. It's cute."

"That's only three reasons."

"Spoken from a woman who hasn't given me one reason yet."

I knocked off the wisps of loose grass that had been blown onto my jeans by a gentle breeze. "You're the only person I know who has never had a cavity."

"That may change if you keep feeding me sweets," Trace interjected. "Go on."

"You don't like being barefoot either, even on the carpet in your own house."

"Which is why we're a perfect match because your mother has sent you more than enough of those silly socks to share with me."

"I love my mommy's socks," I said. "Can I finish?"

Trace zipped his fingers across his lips.

"Now I've lost my train of thought." I leaned back on my elbows and let my head fall back so the sun would warm my face. When I closed my eyes, I felt Trace's presence close to my face. His lips touched mine. Softly. A pause. And then softly again.

"Did that help?" he asked me.

I prayed this wasn't a dream. I prayed that I wasn't really in my bed wearing baggy sweatpants that I fell asleep in after spending all night looking at houses for my client. I opened my eyes slowly.

"I've suddenly remember something else about you," I cooed. "You're a great kisser."

I placed my hand on Trace's neck and pulled him toward me. We stopped as our lips were about to touch. Breathed each other in. This time, I kissed him. I savored Trace's kiss like a sweet peach on a summer's day.

After too long, I pulled my lips away from his. "We—we should *not* do that again," I said, my breath still taken away. "It's too risky and we are two adults trying to live right."

"You're not making it easy. You do realize you're the one who attacked me, right?"

"Attack? You call that an attack?"

"I do." He licked his bottom lip. "I should probably wear protective gear when I'm with you."

I nodded. "You should. The full armor of God. You're gonna need every piece of it to stay a saint.

"Better a saint than a sinner," Trace said. He scooted back from me and drew an imaginary line between us. "I'll stay on my side and you stay on yours. Deal?"

"I'll do my best," I said.

"Do you want reason number four?" Trace asked.

"What is it?" My entire face smiled. I could feel my eyes squint and the full apples of my cheeks rise.

"Because your lips taste like strawberries and they're my favorite fruit."

And peaches were mine.

Chapter 15

Kiysha draped her cotton towel over her neck and lowered the speed on her treadmill until she was walking at a speed comfortable enough for her to cool down. I'd finished giving her every detail about my day out with Trace.

"You should be the first person at the altar tomorrow morning and the last person to leave," she said. "I love a good kiss, but you know how that leads to other things."

"I know, I know," I laughed. "All of that from a kiss. What's wrong with me?"

"Nothing is wrong with you. You're a woman and your libido has been awakened from a long hibernation. At this point, a puff of wind could've done the job."

The man riding the stationary bike beside me had supposedly been wrapped up in watching the multi-view television hanging above our heads, but Kiysha's comment brought a burst of laughter out of him. Kiysha covered her mouth and mouthed, "*My bad.*"

"Every woman needs a crazy girlfriend," I said "You, my dear cousin, are mine."

1.34 miles. I slid my feet out of the straps on the spin cycle I'd been riding. My entire workout session, I'd been ignoring the evil stare of the lady who wanted to claim this particular bike, even though there were three empty and available ones on the next row. Her legs look like the horse's I'd ridden that morning, and she'd nearly nipped my heels trying to get to the bike before me. But I was on a mission. At least for the evening. After my morning rendezvous with Trace, I'd had a sudden spurt of energy. I felt alive. I'd sent a listing of houses to two clients who'd been considerate enough to put their searching on hold until I returned from my self-imposed sabbatical. If my business clients could wait for their house, then surely the exercise fanatic could wait for the bike.

I swept a towel I'd brought from home down the back of my sweaty neck and spotted Bellamy heading upstairs from the first floor of the gym. Downstairs was the free weight area, the group exercise classrooms, and all of the intimidating machines that were being hogged by the muscle heads and the gym regulars.

"That class was exhilarating," Bellamy huffed, pushing back her sweat drenched bangs with an elastic headband. Her face was covered in red splotches. "I'm telling you. You would've loved it."

"Anything that calls for hip gyrating isn't me."

Bellamy patted her abdomen area that I had to admit had flattened nicely over the last three months.

"It's perfect for working your core," she said.

"My core is perfect the way it is," I said. Maybe I'd eaten a few too many cupcakes and had consumed way too much baked bread over the fall and winter months, but now that it was spring, I was hoping my muffin pouch would disappear on its own.

"She's mad because she's one out of the forty-three black girls in the world that doesn't have rhythm," Kiysha joked. "Wait until your wedding reception. You'll see for yourself."

"Come to think of it, I've never seen you dance," Bellamy said. "Is that why?

I pushed my ear buds into my ears even though I didn't have the music on. "Let's keep focused on the task at hand, people. We're here to get fit, not to analyze my dancing skills."

"Or lack thereof," Kiysha said.

I started to pedal again. My legs calves and thighs already felt like Jell-O, but I refused to abandon the cycle just because the lady was still boring a hole through the side of my head. "I know you want to look fabulous in your bridesmaid dress for me, but you could be the next one floating down the altar. I can't wait. I'm so excited for you. This is the re-beginning of something wonderful. And yes, I know I made up a word."

"We're taking it one day at a time," I said, pulling by earbuds out of my ears again.

"You've been growing a friendship. Maybe God wanted it that way between you two from the beginning. It removes all the pressure and you can completely be yourselves. You know he's the one," Bellamy said. She patted her hand over her heart. "You can feel it right here. I know you. I know you've prayed about it on your own, and I'm sure Trace has, too. But you all should pray together now and ask God for the intention of your relationship."

"Listen at little Bellamy acting all ministerial and whatnot," Kiysha smiled. She brought her treadmill to a slow stop. Her breasts nearly fell out of her low cut sports bra as she bent down to tie her shoe. I wasn't the only one who noticed. The man running to her right nearly lost control of his legs.

"And while I'm on a roll, let me address you."

"Me? What did I do?" Kiysha asked.

"It's not what you did, it's what you *don't* do."

Kiysha snatched two antiseptic wipes from the container attached to the side of the machine to wipe down the handlebars of her treadmill. "Enlighten me."

"You should be more open to the kind of man God might send to you. You have this tainted view that because a man has money, or advanced degrees, or is handsome, or can drop a scripture or two on you—that he's the one. What if he makes an honest but humble living as a mechanic or an air conditioner installer? And what if....what if he's not ...how do you usually say it? What if he's not hot chocolate? What if he's cool whip?"

All three of us burst out laughing. "Bellamy, did you say cool whip?" I said.

"I couldn't think of anything else. It sounded good at the time." She turned back to Kiysha. "But anyway. What if?"

"You can't fault me for being attracted to the brothers."

"I'm not faulting you. "I'm saying that God made tons of other flavors. That's all."

"You're right," Kiysha said. "And after today's date with Dr. Phillips, I need to be willing to step out of my comfort zone. Jump out of it."

"What happened?" Bellamy pushed.

I'd slowed my cycling to the point that my legs were barely moving. Now instead of Jell-O, they felt like a ton of bricks had been strapped around my ankles. "Do you really have to recount this story again? It was your decision to go out with him. I merely suggested it," I said, taking the blame off of myself.

Kiysha ignored me. "I'll give you the short version, Bellamy. Doctor Phillips is a psychologist. He spent seventy percent of the time analyzing my childhood and the other thirty percent talking about himself. His boring self. The best thing about my night was the delicious blackened salmon and spinach salad. I mean, it was tasty, but I gave up my entire afternoon for some green leaves and an hour on the shrink's couch."

"Consider it a free meal," Bellamy said. "Do you want to write a review for my blog about it?" Bellamy said, fishing for content.

Kiysha promptly turned her down. "No. I'm trying to think of my own theme for a blog. Do you know how many subscribers Vaughn has now? If she tells everyone who she is, she might actually have become a local celebrity."

"Fifteen minutes of fame isn't worth my dignity," I said, lowering my voice. "Having my love and relationships business broadcast on the web is a bit intrusive."

I could barely push the pedals. I slid off the bike seat but kept my hand on it to stake my claim for the territorial woman who was still seething in the corner.

I gestured for Bellamy and Kiysha to gather around my bike. "A writer from Essence Magazine contacted me through my blog. She's writing an article on sex and the single woman and she wants to interview me—and I can retain my anonymity."

"Sex? She's not going to get very much information from you," Kiysha said. She raised her brows. "Is she?"

"Yeah. Is she?" Bellamy added.

"Not like that," I said, fanning away their foolishness. "I can focus on celibacy."

"Well, don't let her steer you into telling all of your business, anonymity or not," Kiysha warned.

Bellamy patted her cheeks, but it only left white fingerprints in the red splotches on her face that hadn't faded. "I'd definitely do it. This is your chance to represent God and what you stand for. There's something to be said for a woman who wants to enter her marriage with honor."

Kiysha kneeled to tie her shoelace. "It's been too long for me. Something better happen soon before my honor runs out."

"You know what Pastor John always says. 'You can choose the sin, but you can't choose the consequence,'" Bellamy reminded them.

"Amen to that," I said.

We made our way to the locker room to get the belongings we'd all stuffed into one locker. Bellamy's swim suit was hanging on the single hook inside. "I was thinking about taking some laps in the pool," she said. "You guys want to join me?"

Kiysha put her hands on her hips. "I thought I taught you this rule last summer. There are certain things your black girlfriends will and won't do. Do you need a refresher course?"

"Oh wait," Bellamy said, holding up her hair like she was taking a vow. "My black girlfriends will not take unscheduled dips in the pool because it's a hair thing."

"Thank you," Kiysha said. "Now there are exceptions to every black girlfriend rule, but this is the common standard."

"Point taken," Bellamy throwing an amused smile in my direction.

I shook my head. That was only one of the black girlfriend rules that Kiysha called herself teaching Bellamy.

"Enjoy your swim, Bell. I'm going home to relax. Trace is tied up working on a project so before he brought me home, he checked out four movies from Redbox to keep me company."

"Since he's staked his claim again, guess he doesn't want you running the streets."

"Whatever," I said. "I'm enjoying my downtime. In about two weeks, I'll be back on the grind again."

Kiysha threw her gym bag over her shoulder. "See you at church in the morning?"

"Of course you will. Don't be late," I said. "I'll wait for you in the vestibule."

"Better late than never," she said.

"That's what I was thinking today about me and Trace. Better late than never."

Chapter 16

I'd been waiting near the front kiosk of my church's foyer so I could get information about the upcoming women's conference when my phone pinged with a text from Kiysha.

I'm late. See you after church is over.

A greeter with a sunshiny smile brought me a brochure in the growing line of women. My church's annual women's conference was the most popular and highly-attended events of the year. My first year in attendance, I'd met Bellamy, and we hadn't missed one yet. I turned around to head to my usual spot in the sanctuary—left side, second section—and immediately bumped into Trace.

"What are you doing here?" I asked, pleasantly surprised.

"I thought I'd come see you this morning, since I'll be tied up for the rest of the day. I have to meet with my team at one and I'm not sure what the rest of the week's going to look like."

"How thoughtful," I said, wanting to crawl in and hibernate between his arms. "I must be pretty special."

"More than special."

"Can I get a hug? Trace asked.

"Keep it clean, and keep the obligatory space between all body parts. We are in the house of the Lord."

"Tell yourself that," Trace said, though he still hugged me like we were siblings. "I even dressed for your church."

The attire at my church, simply named The Vine, was casual. I couldn't even say business casual since many of our younger congregates attended every Sunday wearing jeans and the popular vintage t-shirts of cartoon characters I'd grown up watching—Grape Ape, Speed Racer and My Little Pony. But despite the laid back atmosphere, I rarely wore jeans. It didn't feel right, especially since my childhood church was a weekly show of our Sunday's best.

Trace fit right in with his khaki pants and aqua blue, polo-style shirt. Very springy. But he was carrying a blazer and even my pastor didn't wear a blazer unless it was a special occasion. Trace's pastor, however, entered the pulpit armed with his big black Bible, a crisp white handkerchief, and a three-piece suit. Mt. Ephraim Baptist was as Southern as sweet tea. They opened their worship services with traditional spirituals. We opened our services with a variety of art forms. Sometimes spoken word, rock, or like this Sunday, we enjoyed being led by our entire Hispanic ministry. *Gloria a dios!*

Trace lost himself in worship, which renewed my attraction for him even more. He wasn't the best singer, but it didn't matter since he could trill his r's like it was his native language. If it hadn't been for the English translations on the side screens, I wouldn't have known what they were saying. "Praise the Lord! *Alabado se el Senor! El Senor is mi fuertza, y mi corazon, an el Confia, de El recibo ayuda!*"

Trace enjoyed Pastor John's sermon. It was evident by the copious notes he'd taken on his phone's notepad. I knew that he'd expect me to visit Mt. Ephraim soon and I'd attend to appease him. But on the three occasions that I'd attended their services on Sunday, I couldn't help but think how I didn't feel the same connection there. His church members welcomed me with open arms and some sweet kisses on my jaw from the elderly women who claimed the second row of pews every single Sunday. They adored Trace and he returned their affection. They'd adopted him as their grandson and he showered compliments and gifts on them on a regular basis. He'd never mentioned it to me, but one of his "grandmothers" had shared with me that he'd treated the entire Seasoned Saints ministry to a brunch at their favorite local buffet. They were his Atlanta family and he'd undoubtedly want to bring me into their fold.

That was a discussion for another day. One day at a time.

"I wish I could see you tomorrow," I said, slightly pouting. Trace had walked me to my car, even though he'd parked on the other side of the building. The traffic exiting was still thick so there was no reason for him to rush out.

"I'll do what I can," he said. "Don't make that face trying to get your way."

"What face?" I asked, innocently.

Trace touched my forehead with his index finger, then slowly traced the silhouette of my face. "You're beautiful."

"You tell me that all the time," I said. I slid my feet out of the low pumps I'd worn and wiggled my toes.

"Because it's true all the time." Trace leaned against my car door. "I have to go. I don't want to, but duty calls. I need to take care of my business."

"As do I," I said. "Kiysha's going to follow me to the house I have to show since I've never met them before."

"That's a good idea. Be safe. I'll see you tomorrow." He kissed his fingertips then touched his fingers to my left cheek, nose, then right cheek. Traced turned and walked away, waving to Kiysha who was parked three spaces away.

When we finally made it out of the parking lot, she shadowed me to a last minute showing I'd agreed to do for one of my fellow agents whose mother had fallen sick in the middle of the night.

I pulled into the circular driveway in front of the house and used the code that Bridgette had texted me to open the lock box and retrieve the key.

From the minute I walked into the expansive foyer, I could see what a steal it was. Hardwood floors spanned from the entry way and into the kitchen. To my right was an area that had probably been used as a sitting room, and to my left were built-in bookcases that were suitable for an office or library. With an airy and open floor plan, I could see the beautiful kitchen and dining room area that boasted floor to ceiling windows. Deals like this were about to become scarce once the market finally took an upswing.

But evidently the seller didn't care about the market forecast. According to Bridgette, he was a recent divorcee whose wife abandoned him for a more affluent man. He wanted no memories of her which is why he wanted to ditch the house as soon as possible and take the loss. Move on.

I shook my head. The seller's heart must've been ripped out and handed to him on the monogrammed silver platter that was still on the stone countertop.

I'd ventured upstairs for a tour when I heard the tap of heavy heels on the downstairs hardwood.

"Hello?" I called out.

"It's the owner," the man's voice said. "I'm going to box up some books and I'll be out of the way in about ten minutes. Is that okay?"

I rounded the corner and was about to bound down the stairwell when the homeowner and I caught a glimpse of each other.

I froze.

He froze.

I could've tipped Roderick over with a feather.

"Vaughn. Wow. I had no idea. Bridgette told me she was sending someone else to show the house, but I had no idea it would be you."

"And trust me, I had no idea you were the owner." I tapped my fingers on the wooden railing and wondered why Kiysha hadn't run in to give me a warning. "Nice place. You're going to make some family real happy, especially with this asking price."

"Somebody deserves to be happy living in it," Roderick said.

Our voices echoed in the emptiness of where his life had once been. His happily ever after didn't end up so happy. Karma. Or better yet, what a man sows, he'll also reap. I wanted to tell Roderick he deserved every piece of heartache he'd been handed, but it wasn't my place to throw salt in his wounds. My complete happiness in myself and his FOR SALE sign in the front yard said enough.

Roderick walked over to the bottom step as if he were waiting for me to descend into his arms. At our wedding, I was supposed to make my entrance from the top of a long winding staircase. I always wondered what I'd feel if our paths were to ever cross again. I'd made a conscious effort to completely remove myself from his life. I cut off communication with his family and with the mutual friends we'd shared. When I returned from "our" honeymoon with Kiysha, I left Roderick responsible for returning the wedding gifts and concentrated on reclaiming my life.

"I've caught your name here and there in some of the Atlanta business magazines. You're doing good for yourself."

"Great," I corrected him. "I'm doing great for myself."

Roderick shoved his hands in his pockets, which pulled his belt line under his growing stomach. He'd put on at least fifteen pounds and I wouldn't be surprised if the stress from his marital problems had driven him to his late night craving of eating Fruit Loops. I guess it had all finally caught up with him.

"You're not married yet?" he asked, glancing at my bare ring finger. "I guess you've been chasing the money and not men."

"I've never chased men," I reminded him. "I get chased. And those who want me finally catch up. Those who aren't worthy will be weeded out. You know the drill."

Roderick scratched the stubble on his chin. "You disappeared. You never gave me a chance to apologize."

There was nothing. Nothing rolled up in my belly or

squeezed my heart when Roderick said those words. *Thank you, Jesus.* My mom had always told me that my complete healing from that heartbreak was possible. It was one hundred percent true. But that didn't mean I was going to stand in this gigantic, empty house and rehash old emotions. His, or mine. This trip was all about business.

"You should go ahead and pack your boxes," I suggested. "The potential buyers might be here any minute." I held onto the handrail as I descended the stairs. "I'll be waiting outside until then."

I closed the door behind me and saved my drama until I reached Kiysha's car. She'd parked at the curb on the street and was so engulfed in playing something on her phone that she didn't notice it was me—and not a cloud—that had blocked her sunlight. I tapped on the window.

"Why do you have such a scowl on your face?" she said, putting her window down.

"Did that guy who came in rub you the wrong way?"

"That guy who came in was Roderick. And he's still in there. You should've given me a heads up."

"If I'd seen who it was, I wouldn't have had to warn you because you and the rest of the neighbors would've heard me beating his little behind and dragging him up and down the sidewalk." Kiysha's neck was in full motion.

I held my hands out and gestured for her to calm

down. I smirked. "He's not that little anymore. You might not be able to drag him as far as you think you can."

"And his extra weight is probably all in his big head."

Kiysha reached over to the floor of the passenger's seat for her high-heeled shoes. I didn't know if she was planning to wear them or use them as weapons, but I pushed my weight against the car door when she tried to open it.

"I can handle this," I said. "We're in a quiet, respectable neighborhood. Act civilized."

"I am acting civilized," Kiysha spurted. "And it's my civic duty to beat his behind. And his wife, too. I bet that little heifer was in on it from the beginning."

"Really, Kiysha? It's been five years. You shouldn't be this amped up."

"Pray for me. I need Jesus." Kiysha stopped pushing against the car door. She picked up the women's conference brochure that had been tucked in her Bible. "He's got me sweating and carrying on out here. He's making my fake eyelash come off." She blinked her right eye. "So what's the news?"

"Roderick is divorced now," I waited to see her reaction.

"You know what? There are some things I want to say, but because it's Sunday, I'm going to leave it alone." Kiysha tuned her radio to a gospel music station. "I need just a little more Jesus to soothe this savage beast," she sang.

I stepped closer to Kiysha's car as a pick-up truck approached a bend in the road. "Maybe you should give Dr. Phillips a call so he can diagnose the cause of your residual anger."

"Don't start with me," she said. Kiysha turned her key in the ignition and shifted into drive.

"Where are you going?" I asked.

"Into the driveway. Beside Roderick's car. At the very least, I can give him the evil eye when he comes out."

"I'm sure he'll be shaking in his wing-tipped shoes," I said, walking behind Kiysha's car as she crept up the driveway and did exactly what she said she would. I opened her passenger's door and slid in.

"In all seriousness, are you okay?" Kiysha asked. "Forget Roderick. You're the one who means the most to me.

"I couldn't be better," I said, meaning it. "Trace likes my little crooked toenail, he knows that pecans itch the roof of my mouth, and he thinks my kisses taste like strawberries. I'm good. Correction. I'm great. That's what I told Roderick, and that's what I would tell anybody who asked."

The front door swung open and Roderick exited, carrying his box of books. The bottom of the cardboard bulged, threating to spill the contents across the stone-patterned pavement.

"Hmmph," Kiysha grunted. "Aren't you glad God can see the entire picture of our lives?"

"So glad," I said.

Kiysha kept her eyes on him, not bothering to pretend like she wasn't staring him down. He grinned like a Cheshire cat at her, and tipped his chin up to signal hello, but Kiysha didn't blink or crack a smile.

"Are you going to tell Trace that you saw him?" she asked.

"Probably. I have nothing to hide."

"Did he ever say anything else about that Stephanie chick?" Kiysha asked me.

"Nothing. And I haven't asked. I don't have to worry about her. I know Trace is mine."

Chapter 17

I had no desire to be with Roderick in the least bit, but seeing him had pulled some of our times together out of my memory bank. Times I'd long forgotten about until today. After I returned from the house showing with Bridgette's clients, I'd retreated to my balcony with an antique bird cage I'd discovered and a piece of sandpaper. The do-it-yourself wanna-be in me planned to use it as a planter or a lamp, I hadn't quite decided. But as I scraped away the peeling paint and rust on the metal cage bars, I thought of the time we had a soap and water fight when we'd been washing his car one Sunday afternoon. I thought about our first month dating when he'd sent me a singing telegram to work for my birthday. I thought about how my life might be different if he hadn't done what he'd done. If I had been enough for him.

I'd called Trace twice in the last hour, but his phone

went directly to voicemail like it had been turned off. I thought about calling his office phone, but I didn't want to disturb him when my only reason for calling was to hear his voice. He finally called me close to midnight.

"I've been waiting to hear your voice," I told him, without even saying hello.

"I'm sorry. It's been a long day. And a long night," he said. I could hear the grogginess in his voice.

"You sound tired."

"More mentally than anything, but I need to get some sleep so I can get up and do it all again tomorrow." He paused to yawn. "You sound wide awake. What are you doing?"

"Making a grilled cheese sandwich, believe it or not," I admitted. If it hadn't been for the food show I'd been watching where the host wanted to find the nation's best grilled sandwich, I wouldn't be standing over the stove with a spatula in hand. The thought of warm toasted bread and melted cheese had pulled me out of bed.

"That's reason number five that we should be together."

I pressed the spatula against my sandwich until I heard a soft sizzle. I flipped the sandwich over to the browned side with the perfect amount of butter seeping through. "You think we should be together because I know how to cook grilled cheese?"

"No, I think we should be together because I like eating grilled cheese sandwiches at night. What would make it even better was if you had a tall glass of orange juice."

"And I do," I said. "Extra calcium and a little pulp."

"You know a grilled cheese sandwich isn't good unless you take it off the heat right before it starts to burn. It has to have that grilled taste."

"Look," I said. "I'm the master at grilled cheese. I made them almost every morning in high school."

"Reason number six," Trace said. "If you had one bite of your sandwich left, you'd give it to me."

I pulled my pan from the stove's eye and let my sandwich finish cooking from the heat still trapped on the non-stick surface. "I don't know about that," I said, pulling a plate and glass from the cabinet. "The last bite is one of the best."

"Then let me take the first bite."

Knock. Knock. Knock.

"You are not," I said.

"I am. Open the door, Vaughn."

"I can't," I said.

"Why?"

"Because I'm not dressed appropriately. Have you forgotten it's almost midnight?"

"Men don't usually say this to women, but put some clothes on."

"I'm going to unlock the door, but don't come in until you count to ten."

"You better move fast," Trace said. "I'm counting by fives."

I skirted down the hallway to the room and snatched open the bottom drawer of my dresser where I stuffed what I called my house clothes—things I couldn't bear to throw away because they were so comfortable, but items I'd never be seen wearing in public. These were the clothes appropriate for Trace's impromptu visit since my other attire for nighttime was too short and skimpy. And God knows that's the last thing we needed.

I stepped out of my shorty-shorts and tank top and pulled on my CAU alumni t-shirt with the coordinating sweatpants that had a faded panther crawling down the left leg. When I returned to the living room, Trace had poured two tall glasses of orange juice. He looked as comfortable as I did in his own pair of grey sweatpants and a t-shirt that had seen better days.

"At church, I told you I'd try to see you tomorrow." He held up his wrist to show me the face of his watch. "It's tomorrow."

That was Trace. I shouldn't have been surprised, but the things he did melted my heart like it was the first time. We sat across the kitchen table from each other, and although I offered Trace the first bite of my grilled cheese, he'd turned it down since he'd eaten a late night dinner of Chinese take-out.

"Thank you for coming by," I said. "But you look tired," I said.

"Because I am," Trace said. "It's starting to make me think I should've taken that time off."

"You should have. If I've learned one thing, it's that work will always be there." I took a long drink of juice. "Work constantly calls my name but I've been trying my best not to get sucked in. It's hard."

"Because you love what you do," Trace said. He pointed at the corner of my sandwich. "Let me have that bite right there."

I held my sandwich out so he could bite off the side of it. "You're right. You might need to let go of baking and specialize in grilled cheese."

"I wouldn't go that far," I said. "But it is good, isn't it? The perfect combination of cheese and butter."

Trace's pop-up appearance meant more than he knew. Even though we'd never completely pulled ourselves out of each other's lives, tonight was another example of how much he cared about me. It confirmed how much I'd never stopped caring about him either.

"Do you pray for me?" I asked him.

"All the time," Trace said about him. "I pray for you and I pray about you. I pray about us."

"What do you pray?"

"I pray that God would direct our lives and show both of us how we can be a blessing to each other. And as much as I love you I've prayed that if I'm not His best for you, then give me the courage to walk away. But the more I prayed, the stronger my love grew."

"I saw Roderick today," I blurted out. "He happened to be the owner of the house I had to show today. Total coincidence." I could tell that it took Trace's mind a moment to register the significance of that name, but once it did, he still didn't seem to have much of a reaction.

"And?" Trace asked.

"And he's getting a divorce. That's why his house is up for sale."

"That's too bad," Trace said. He stood up so he could clear the table of my empty plate, then he rinsed our glasses and placed them in the sink.

Trace knew our history, yet he didn't ask about our conversation. If he wondered if we'd exchanged numbers or promised to meet again at a later date, he didn't ask. If it crossed Trace's mind about if I longed for a second chance with Roderick, he didn't let it be known. Roderick was my history, and Trace planned to keep it that way.

We found our way to the sofa and sat on opposite ends. I stretched my legs across the length of the sofa that comfortably sat three people, and he pulled my feet on top of his legs. He strummed his fingers across my zebra-printed socks and sang the chorus to "Wild Thing."

At one o'clock, we were playing a session of "name that tune" based on songs from the nineties and at two-thirty in the morning, we'd watched two old episodes of *I Love Lucy*.

I squinted my eyes open at the soft tug to my little toe.

"Vaughn, I need to go home. Get up so you can lock the door," Trace whispered.

"What time is it?"

"Five-thirty. And the rest of Atlanta is about to wake up."

Trace held out his hands so I could catch hold of them. He pulled me until I was sitting upright.

"Good morning," I said, with my face turned slightly away from him in case full-blown morning breath had settled in. I'd fallen asleep without brushing my teeth of the remains of the grilled cheese sandwich and orange juice. The area under Trace's eyes was slightly swollen from lack of sleep.

"Reason number six," Trace said softly. "I know every day that the sun is going to set and every morning that the sun is going to rise. And I know that with every sunset I want to go to bed with you in arms, and with every sunrise I want to wake up to your face."

My heart fluttered, but I still turned away.

"You don't have to say anything. I don't even expect you to because it's all about one day at a time for you. But I can't help it. It's the romantic man in me. I get it from my Dad and I'm not ashamed of it."

Trace kissed my knuckles. If it was truly possible for a person's heart to melt, mine would've leaked from my pores.

Chapter 18

"By this time next year, you'll be married," Bellamy said.

"It's taken you over a year to plan your wedding. What makes you so sure I'm going to run down the aisle, if it even comes to that?"

"Oh, it's definitely coming to that. And take it from me," Bellamy said. "Skip the theatrics. This wedding has been more trouble than it's worth. Invest the money or take a fabulous honeymoon to Europe. Whether you get married in a breath-taking cathedral or at the courthouse, you'll still be the Mr. and Mrs."

I put a calming hand on Bellamy's shoulder. "Take a deep breath, Bell," I said. I knew when my friend was overwhelmed. She rambled and picked at the cuticles on her thumbs. "I've planned a wedding before. It didn't lead to marriage, but I've still planned a wedding."

Bellamy sat on one of the ultra mod sofas in the

bedroom staging area. IKEA was usually our Wednesday morning place to unwind, test our designing eye, and grab cheap hot dogs. She rested her elbows on her knees and massaged her fingers into her scalp. I allowed her to be with her own thoughts until she looked up at me about two minutes later.

"Are you alright?" I asked her.

"I am now," Bellamy said. "You're right. I needed to breathe. It's been stressful trying to incorporate two cultures into one wedding. This ceremony is going to be like three hours long and everyone is going home with an upset stomach when we mish mash all of these different kinds of food we're going to stuff into their stomachs. I swear our mothers have joined forces with one mission to constantly harass us."

"You are marrying Esteban. Do whatever is going to make the two of you happy. Everyone else will follow suit. They will have no choice. What are they going to do? Not show up at the wedding?"

"*Están volviendo loco*," Bellamy said.

"I'm impressed," I laughed, holding out a hand to help her up. "All I heard was the word crazy."

"I'm finally starting to love learning Spanish. I want to surprise Esteban and recite our vows in Spanish."

"Now that will make him cry," I said. "We're all going to cry. I'll need to stuff extra tissues down the middle of the bouquets."

Bellamy picked up a pillow patterned in yellow and

red flowers and held it out in front of her. She'd placed herself on a strict budget that prohibited her from making any purchases unless they were related to the wedding, but Bellamy loved spring and flowers as much as I loved cupcakes.

"I'm surprised Trace didn't stay with you and watch the sunrise this morning," she said, opening that conversation back up again. "Tell me more. I know he did something romantic."

When Trace had been leaving my apartment, Bellamy had been heading for an early morning workout at the gym. She'd called me fifteen minutes later so I could assure her that we'd kept our hands—and lips— off of each other. I'd wanted to kiss Trace. I'd wanted to taste the peaches, but I didn't even attempt it. I'd walked him to the door, accepted a kiss on my cheek, and closed the door behind him.

"He does romantic things. He says romantic things. Him showing up at my door because he promised to 'see me tomorrow' was romantic enough."

"I love my Esteban and I wouldn't trade him for the world, but he could use some lessons in the romance department. He tries though, and that's all I can ask."

"No man is the total package," I said. "Trace has his five go-to meals that he can cook and he throws everything else on the grill. After that he's lost. I've eaten Esteban's *arroz con pollo* and *camarones en cerveza*." I kissed my fingers to my lips. "You may have to heat things up in the bedroom, but Esteban's got the kitchen covered."

Bellamy swiveled her hips in the way she'd shown me she'd been practicing her *bomba* dance, another tradition they planned to incorporate in the reception. "I can heat the kitchen, too. And the closet and the guest room."

"Okay, okay. Your time is coming," I said.

"Yours, too. And enjoy the ride."

I took a deep breath. "This ride is going at the speed of light."

"Then hold on," Bellamy said. She wrapped her arm around my shoulder as we browsed the aisles of the new spring collection of dinnerware. I ended up buying four place settings of ceramic plates and bowls in a tangerine color that I couldn't resist, and pushed Bellamy out the doors before she bought some very unnecessary kitchen storage containers.

After a quick trip to a local nursery to buy a pothos ivy plant for my refurbished bird cage, Bellamy headed back to our area of town to catch a nap before it was time for her to pull an evening shift, and I headed towards Trace's office with his favorite iced mocha coffee.

I chose the perfect spot in the lot to park my car, so that when he looked out of the window from his eighth floor office, he'd be able to spot me. However, Trace didn't answer his office line or his cell phone, so I left a message for him to call me when he had a chance. So much for my surprise.

I took a quick sip of his iced coffee, assuming he was tied down in meetings and conference calls. That was my assumption until….

….until I saw Trace getting out of a red convertible. With a woman in the driver's seat. A gorgeous woman. It was Stephanie. Of course, I couldn't be for sure since I'd never seen her, but she looked like a Stephanie.

Trace leaned over and gave her a hug. It was quick. Fairly innocent. But they'd probably already had a more passionate embrace elsewhere in the shadows of a restaurant. Trace enjoyed romantic, high-end places. And all of this happened while I was eating a hot dog at IKEA.

I wished I could hear the words he was saying as he opened his car door, because the woman threw her head back in laughter. Trace was funny, but not that funny. She patted him on the shoulder before he got out and disappeared behind the tinted glass doors. I waited another five minutes and tried both of his numbers again. Voice mail.

I opened my driver's door and dumped the iced coffee out in the parking lot. *God, I did not give this relationship another chance so I could go through drama like this. That's why I walked away the first time*, I thought. It was better to leave a man before they had the chance to break your heart. And seeing Trace and Stephanie had placed a crack in mine.

Trace didn't return my call until late that night, and of course being the somewhat stubborn woman that I am sometimes, I ignored his call. After two unreturned texts to me, he probably assumed that I was asleep. All afternoon, I'd busied myself with finding options for some real estate continuing education classes, and looked over the career plan I'd drafted at the beginning of the year. Bellamy had said a year from now I'd be walking down the aisle, but that was the furthest thing from my mind. Stop the thrilling ride. Stop the romance.

There was more than enough going on in my life that could keep me preoccupied with things other than love. Other than Trace. I wanted to take the exam for my broker's license and I wanted to make enough sales by the end of the year to break my record in Atlanta's Multi-Million Dollar Sales Club.

I was painting my nails a new shade of mint green when Kiysha knocked on my door. She barged inside talking about her two disastrous Mix & Mingle dates. There was Don Juan who'd claimed to work in the entertainment industry but was actually a stripper, and Terrell was a washed out basketball player who was still living his hoop dreams under his mother's roof.

I'd tried to keep my tears from falling, but they dropped one by one. Then in twos. And then the flood came. With no words. I needed to cry.

"Trust me. It was nothing," Kiysha said after I'd told her all that had transpired. "If you look for something wrong, you'll find it," she said.

"I didn't look for it. It found me," I'd said before I retreated to my bedroom. She worked on the puzzle still scattered on my coffee table and I fumed alone in my room.

"Trace call?"

"Of course, but I ignored his call and both of his texts."

"Don't be like that. You've got it wrong, Vaughn."

"Don't worry. I'll call him back in a few days after he's had time to brew about things. I'll let him put two and two together. I'll let him realize he's been caught."

"Caught doing what?" Kiysha exclaimed. She turned my laptop towards her and furiously pecked on my keyboard. When she turned it back around, she'd pulled up my blog. I'd updated it two days ago with my details about my horseback riding date with Trace and his impromptu midnight visit and hadn't looked at it since.

"Three hundred and twenty four comments. If you don't want Trace, believe me there's a woman who does."

I scrolled through the comments. "*Finally a winner.*" "*Who is the guy and where can I find one just like him?*" "*After dates from hell, it sounds like this might be a match made in heaven. Keep us posted.*"

"If you can't take my word that you're jumping to

conclusions, why don't you ask your followers what they think?"

"Hold up," I said, looking at the counter at the bottom of my page. "I have fourteen thousand, three hundred and thirty-four subscribers? Amazing. That's a whole lot of nosey people."

"No. That's a whole lot of hopeless romantics. Some men of course who want the chance to woo you off your feet, and some women who want your throw-aways, but all of them are rooting for the man that loves you. And they don't even know that the two of you have history."

"I'm not asking advice from complete strangers," I said, fanning my nails in the air.

"You don't have to ask for advice if you ask Trace. You haven't given the man a chance to explain."

"Fine. I'll call him tomorrow."

"Okay," Kiysha said. "And did I tell you I'm crashing here tonight? The crazy couple who lives above me is taking some hip hop line dancing class and they spend half the night doing the wobble and cupid shuffle when I'm trying to sleep."

"If you keep staying here you're going to owe me half the rent."

"The advice I give is priceless," Kiysha told me. "But if that's not enough, I'll make you sweet potato pancakes in the morning."

"Thanks, roomie," I conceded.

"You know if you're hard up for money, we could

charge Dr. Govan Phillips to advertise on your site. Some of the people leaving these comments have some serious issues and we can work it out so we get a cut as a referral fee."

I tried my best to kick a pillow in her direction. "Good-night, Kiysha. Love you, girl."

"Love you, too. And get a good night's sleep. You're going to need it," she said before she abruptly closed the door.

"What do you mean by that?" I yelled out.

As usual, she ignored me.

☙ ❧

I spent most of the night star-gazing out of my bedroom window, nevertheless my rest was peaceful. I'd talked to God in the middle of the night and undoubtedly felt His presence. He spoke words deep into my spirit and breathed life into my soul. I needed it like a deer needs water from a stream. God had blessed me in so many ways and I counted Trace as one of those blessings. Whatever Trace's explanation, I knew that God wanted the best for me.

I felt like I'd just fallen into a deep sleep when I thought I heard the faint ringing of my home phone. It took me a moment to realize that it wasn't the background noise from the local morning news. I flipped over on my back and stretched and contorted my body until I could find the phone without opening my eyes.

Only Meta Holiday and telemarketers called my home phone line.

"Good morning." Trace's voice welcomed me.

"Hi," I said. I cleared my throat. "What time is it?"

"About six-twenty. I tried to call you a couple of times last night but you didn't answer."

"I was busy working," I justified. "You know how it is."

"I do," Trace said. We paused. The silence between us long. "Can I take you to lunch?"

"We need to talk," I said. Six-twenty was too early to address the issues I wanted to discuss, but by lunch I'd definitely have my thoughts and my emotions together.

"Yes, we do need to talk. So lunch?"

My mind changed now that Trace had turned the tables on me.

"We might as well talk now if it's important," I urged him.

"Lunch would be better."

"But you'll have to rush through lunch and get back to work."

"Don't worry about that," Trace said. "I'll pick you up at eleven so we can beat the lunch crowd."

"That's fine. See you then."

"Okay," I said, followed by a yawn. "I'm going back to sleep for a while. I'll see you at eleven."

I powered on my cell phone and set the alarm for ten o'clock. I could hear Kiysha preparing for work in the guest hallway bathroom. Her beauty regimen would last another hour based on her normal shower, prep, and makeup routine. As long as she factored my sweet potato pancakes into her morning plan, I'd be fine.

I sent her a text message: *Don't wake me. C urself out. Leave my pancakes.*

She answered: *U r a meanie. Love u anyway.*

I closed my eyes half-listened to the voice of the CBS meteorologist promising sunshine and seasonably warm weather for the next five days. By next week, all of the house hunters who'd been hibernating since winter would want to look for dream home and I'd be there to service them. My spring break was officially coming to an end.

When the news team returned with an update of the public corruption case against a local official, I turned off the television, and lowered the ringer on my cell. So low, unfortunately, that I didn't hear the alarm I'd set to wake me at ten.

"Vaughn," Trace said when I picked up my home line again. "Are you still asleep?"

"Yes. What's up? Do you have to cancel?" I asked, without opening my eyes.

"No. I'm on my way to your house. It's ten forty-five."

"You're kidding me."

"I wish I was."

"I apologize. Can we go to dinner instead?" I decided.

"That's not going to work. I have reservations."

"Can't you change them? Or change the place? Seven will work for me."

"It's not that easy, babe," Trace said. I heard the slightest bit of frustration in his voice.

"I'm just waking up. I can't get ready in fifteen minutes."

"Reason number seven. You're already beautiful. You don't need to do much."

"But in fifteen minutes?" It's a sin to ask a woman to get ready that fast."

"Then twenty minutes," Trace said. "I really want to see you."

"I really wanted to see you yesterday, too," I said, allowing the scene to replay in my mind. Of course the emotions came with it, but I stopped. Breathed. And I got it together. "I wanted to surprise you but I was the one that ended up surprised."

"How? You came to my job? You didn't tell me that."

"Because I left after I saw your lunch date dropped you off in her red convertible."

"Did you also happen to see Felicia's wedding ring? Her husband, Jerry—one of the minister's at my church—slid it on her finger about twenty years ago. You've met them before when we went to their house for her surprise birthday party. And her surprise gift—the red convertible."

I was speechless and stunned out of embarrassment into silence. Felicia and Jerry. They'd given me a referral for a client who ended up buying a home in the Johns Creek area.

"I rode with her to look at a Movado watch she wanted to buy for Jerry. She knows how much I love watches and she wanted a second opinion since she was about to drop some good money on it."

I was an idiot. An emotional idiot. "I'll be ready when you get here," I said, jumping out of bed.

"I've never given you a reason not to trust me, and I'm not going to start now. I don't play games and my mama taught me better than to play with a woman's heart. I know what that'll get you. I learned from my frat brothers' experiences. Slit tires. Intentional overdoses. Rocks busted through windows. I'm not about that life. Your cousin is Kiysha, so I know you've got some crazy in you."

"You're going to get enough talking about my family," I told him. "You've been forewarned." I walked into my closet and found the simplest outfit that didn't need ironing. Since Trace had made reservations, I opted on a casual pair of slacks instead of jeans, and paired them with a camisole and soft-yellow, short-sleeved cardigan. In eighteen minutes I was answering the door.

"Hi, babe," Trace said, pecking my forehead. "We need to get going." He took my hand and moved me from in front of the entry way closet where I'd been standing. He opened the closet and rolled out my weekender bag.

"What are you doing? Who put that in there?"

"Kiysha," Trace answered. "No more questions."

He slid my key ring out of my hand. "What's the alarm code?" he asked.

I robotically punched in the code without answering. He'd never known that the code was the month and day of our first date. "You have to tell me something. Anything." I said.

"Anything?" We stepped out into the hallway. Trace locked the door. "How about this? This is only the beginning."

Chapter 19

A wave of exhilaration rushed over me as we rode the elevator down to the lobby. I eased my hand inside of Trace's and let my head rest on the side of his arm. The doors slid open when we reached the third floor and my resident fitness conscious, Helene, power walked inside to join us.

"Here you are again. The cutest couple in the world," she gushed, over the music that I could hear coming from her earbuds. "Man, it brightens my day to see you guys. One day I'm going to have a love like that."

Helene marched in place and pumped her arms back and forth. "Taking a trip?"

"Something like that," Trace answered, being careful not to reveal his plan.

I wondered where we were headed. Overnight at the Evergreen Resort at Stone Mountain? Chateau Elan? A bed and breakfast? A cabin in the Tennessee mountains?

All options I'd considered for my private birthday giveaway.

"Have fun," Helene said, as the elevator doors opened to the lobby.

As I walked out into the May sun, a driver stepped out of a black town car waiting at the curb. He walked around the back of the car holding a sign that said, VAUGHN HOLIDAY.

"Oh, this is too much," I gushed. "Front door service and everything. A girl could get used to this."

"You should," Trace said, leaving my weekender bag on the curb for the driver to handle. I slid across the leather seat to make space for Trace on the rear passenger's side.

"I'm not going to ask you a single thing," I said.

"Good," Trace said. "And that reverse psychology doesn't work on me."

I tapped the driver on the shoulder. "Excuse me, sir, but where are we headed?"

He turned his head slightly without taking his eyes off the road. "I've been given strict instructions to ignore any and all of your questions," he chuckled.

"And you've earned an extra tip for that," Trace said.

I poked his side with my elbow. "Whatever."

"Reason number eight." Trace said. "Neither of us give up easily."

"You definitely don't," I said. "Hold on a second. I need to send a message to a sneaky little cousin."

U r n for it.

Kiysha responded. *U don't scare me. Have the time of ur life. U deserve it.*

Look in my pantry behind the aluminum foil. Yummy. And don't touch the doll house.

I'd just sent the text message when Trace took the phone out of my hand and hit the camera icon. He reversed the camera so he could take a picture of us, then sent it to Kiysha. I had to agree with Helene. We did look adorable together.

Trace's cell rang. "I'm sorry, baby, this is work. They're only supposed to call me if it's absolutely necessary so let me see what's going on," Trace said. He picked up my hand and kissed the palm before answering. Our fingers twined as I daydreamed out the window and he put out fires at work. We whizzed through downtown Atlanta and past the exits leading to Langford Parkway and East Point when I realized we were headed to the airport.

"We're leaving Atlanta?" I asked. "We're leaving Atlanta," I said, changing it to a statement.

Trace slid his cell phone back into his front pocket but didn't acknowledge my discovery. The driver glanced at me through the review mirror, smiling at me with his eyes.

"You've pulled off some pretty crazy things since I've known you, but this by far is probably the craziest," I said.

We finally entered the airport property and followed the signs to the North Terminal.

Our car eased over to the curb in the drop-off area. I waited on the sidewalk while Trace accepted our bags from the trunk, then tipped the driver.

"The answer to this mystery is drawing closer," I said.

"What's the big deal? We're going to lunch," Trace mused.

"Some lunch," I said, following him to the security line. We circled through the empty maze of partitions. Travel was light today, at least at this hour.

I fiddled in my wallet for my license, knowing I'd have to produce it before entering the area for bag inspection. Trace handed the first agent his cell phone so she could match our identifications with the e-tickets.

"New York, huh?" she said with a thick Southern accent. "You can keep it. Folks up there are mean. They always talk about how much better New York is in Atlanta. If that's the case, why do they keep moving to Georgia?" She slit her eyes. "You're not from New York, are you?"

"No," Trace answered.

I was still reveling over my surprise to indulge in any other conversations. The Big Apple. The concrete jungle. The place were dreams are made. I hadn't been to New York in almost five years when Kiysha had dragged me there to experience the shopping.

We'd worn the wrong shoes. Fashionable, but nowhere near practical for traipsing long distances with handfuls of shopping bags. We were confused by the subway and irritated at the traffic, but when it was all said and done we'd had a blast.

"I don't know what our plans are, but the last time I went to New York, me and Kiysha painted the town red."

"I won't even ask how it went down," Trace said. "But it's no big deal. We're going for lunch."

"Right. Lunch," I said, hesitantly sliding off my shoes for the pat down through security. Trace unzipped the front of my weekender bag and handed me a pair of footies.

"Kiysha said you'd want these."

"She was right," I said, sliding them on quickly in an effort to fight away all of the foot fungus that lurked in public places.

We were held up slightly at the security checkpoint since Trace forgot to remove his belt. Consequently, he received a thorough body groping from the TSA agent.

"How did you enjoy that?" I laughed.

"The most action I've had in a long time," he said.

After a short ride to our boarding gate and having our choice of seats in our section, I finally had the chance to assess what Kiysha had packed in my baggage. Along with jeans and the blouse I'd purchased on my Mix & Mingle date with Huggy Bear, were a little black dress and my go-to pair of stilettos. I didn't know how far those were going to get me in New York, but at least I'd look sexy. However, in true Kiysha fashion, she'd also packed a pair of foldable shoes that I could tuck into my purse for foot emergencies. Other than that, there was a pair of comfy pajamas and a casual outfit for my return. Inside the jewelry clutch, she'd tucked a small pair of silver hoops, a Tiffany chain bracelet (a birthday gift from Trace), and a delicate silver ring with a cross that I sometimes wore on my left ring finger as a vow of purity. *I hear you, Kiysha.*

"So did Kiysha do okay with packing your clothes or are we going to have to an impromptu shopping spree?"

"She did great. You know my girl. She never disappoints when it comes to looking good."

Trace propped his ankle across his knee and sunk deep into the blue leather chairs. He blew out a long stream of air. "You know this excursion is really for me."

"I appreciate your letting me come along for the ride."

"No problem. Anytime," he said, peeking through one of his closed eyes so he could see my expression. I stuck out my tongue at him.

The gate attendant began to announce boarding for Flight #1586 headed to New York.

"We'll be in first class next time," Trace said.

"Right about now I would ride on the wing of the plane," I said, leaning in to plant a kiss on his cheek. "Thank you."

"Thank you for giving us a chance again," Trace said. "You won't regret it."

"I know I won't," I said, revealing my heart. My voice dropped to a whisper. "Thank you for being a man of valor who doesn't have to chase behind every woman with a nice behind and a smile. Like Stephanie."

"How do you know what her behind looks like?" he said.

"I don't. I wanted to see what you were going to say."

"I'd never tell you what I thought about another woman's behind," Trace said. "Even if it was nice and plump."

This time I punched him with more force. He folded in half like I'd actually put enough force behind it to hurt.

"I'm calling security," Trace said.

"You're going to need them. And tell them to bring back up."

Trace helped me to my feet when the gate attendant called for our section. The plane was only half-way full, but was still stuffy and muggy like a team of sweaty football players had exited before we boarded.

I took the window seat on our row and looked out to see the baggage handlers hustling to load the bottom of the plane so we could prepare for takeoff. I closed the window shade, and rested my head on the back of the seat.

Trace used his hand to gently pull my head onto his shoulder.

"I'm excited and sleepy at the same time."

"Finish your nap," Trace suggested. "We have a full day."

So I did. I was still hovering in a drowsy state when the pilot announced takeoff, but once we leveled off above the clouds, I succumbed to the sandman dancing over my head. I didn't rouse again until Trace softly squeezed my knee.

"Wake up, sleepyhead. We're in the Big Apple."

"Don't mention any food right now," I said. "I'm starving."

Trace handled me a miniscule packet of pretzels that they must've passed out while I was snoozing. "We're here for lunch, so you'll eat soon."

We'd carried our luggage aboard so we bypassed baggage claim and headed for ground transportation. We hustled through LaGuardia, along with the other arriving and departing passengers who seemed to be in a rush to get somewhere. Trace signaled to a driver in the parking lot of cabs, but his waving hand set off a musical honking of horns. Taxi drivers stuck their heads out of the window and honked frantically to indicate their availability.

I stopped, unsure of which direction to turn.

"This way, babe," Trace said, pulling me to the right.

The taxi driver jumped out of his cab and popped the

trunk. He hurried over to Trace and took the handles of our bags out of his hands.

"Let's roll," Trace said, opening the back of the cab.

The inside smelled like a mix of motor oil, onions and the citrus-scented air freshener sticks shoved in the grooves of all of the front vents.

"Where are you headed?" the driver asked in and African accent so heavy, I initially thought he was speaking in his native tongue.

"The Algonquin," Trace said, cracking the window so we could both get a breath of fresh air. It wasn't like Georgia air for sure, but it was better than being closed up in our current situation.

"Pray for light traffic," Trace said as our taxi joined the bumper to bumper race to exit the airport.

"What brings you to our city?" our driver asked. "Business or pleasure?" He was paying more attention to me and Trace than he did to the traffic.

"We came to eat lunch," Trace said nonchalantly.

"Really? From where?"

"From Atlanta," I answered. "Can you believe he brought me all the way here to eat?"

The taxi driver threw his head back and bellowed a deep, hearty laugh. He held his hand up and rubbed his fingers together. "Big spender," he said. "One day, I'll be like you."

His toothy smile covered his face. I knew exactly what that meant. He was expecting a huge tip.

Even with the traffic jam into the city, time flew by. Our driver, a Nigerian named Ajani, entertained us with the stories of the passengers he'd driven since his shift started at six o'clock that morning. In his own words, he'd dropped off a rich woman with so many wrinkles she looked like an elephant, and two teenage boys who claimed they were going to be the world's next greatest music producers. The stories went on for thirty-five minutes to the point that I was able to ignore my grumbling stomach.

Trace encouraged Ajani's foolishness, which probably brought out more exaggeration than necessary in the stories. I wondered what he'd say about us.

"Here we are," Ajani said. "Your castle." He pointed down the street. "Walk that way for seven minutes and you'll be in the middle of Time Square."

"Thank you," I said, getting out. I was thankful to be able to stretch my legs. I looked out over the landscape of New York City. I was in New York for lunch. This was crazy. This was beautiful. This was love.

"Do you want a reason?" I said to Trace. I walked up close to him, not worrying about the pedestrians pushing past us. This concrete sidewalk was our piece of the world.

"Because when you smile, I smile, too. Because I love watching you, even when you don't know I am. And because nothing about your love for me has been ordinary. And because you'd fly me to New York to show me." I wrapped my arms around Trace's waist, but stopped him before he did the same to me.

"Hold on to those bags," I said. "I've heard New Yorkers can run pretty fast."

Trace kissed the top of my head. "That was four reasons."

"And I always have more."

Trace looked upward. "God, I am so glad those Mix & Mingle dates were a disaster."

"Yes, you better thank God," I said, leading the way into The Algonquin. "Because if I had a thing for older men, I'd be cuddling up with Huggy Bear right about now."

I found a comfortable spot on the lush seating in the lobby and waited for Trace to check us in. I didn't have to ask if he'd reserved two rooms because I knew he had. On a day like this, with a love feeling like this, it was extremely necessary to have concrete walls between us. And a deadbolt. He returned with two key cards, and then led us to a bank of elevators that took us up to our rooms on the eighth floor.

"We'll put our bags in the room and head back downstairs to the restaurant."

Trace opened the door, pulled it wide....and I shrieked.

"Mom. Jazzy P. What are you guys doing here?"

Like a child after the first day of kindergarten, I ran into my mother's arms. I hadn't expected to cry, but with the emotions overwhelming me since I first boarded the plane in Atlanta, I couldn't contain the tears.

"Trace, I don't know what you've done, but you have my baby crying. And this one is like her mama. Tough. Vaughn never cries."

I wiped under my eyes with my fingers, thankful that I'd been in too much of a rush to put on mascara. "Tell me about it," I sniffed. "I never, never, never would've expected you to be here."

My mama put her hands on her hips. No wonder she was adamant about wearing a bathing suit. She looked marvelous. Her weekly trips to the swimming pool had toned her arms. I could see the sculpting of tiny muscles on her bare arms, courtesy of her silk sleeveless shirt.

"Wait, weren't you supposed to be going on a surprise trip, too?"

"This is it. Trace talked to Jazzy P. Evidently they didn't trust that I wouldn't spill the beans."

"Not only would you spill the beans, you'd dump out the whole pot," Jazzy P said, rubbing his stomach. My mother may have been shrinking, but Jazzy P was expanding. I leaned into his embrace.

"So you all are joining us to eat?"

"Of course," my mom exclaimed. "We didn't fly all the way from across the country for you two love birds to leave us cooped up in this hotel room." She clasped her hands together. "And the Lion King, tonight? Honey, I am all about this fabulous life."

I turned to Trace. "Surprise," he said.

"I told you," Jazzy P said. "She dumps the entire pot over."

My mother picked up a light sweater that was draped across a wing-backed chair. "How was I supposed to know that was a surprise, too?" She rubbed lip balm across her lips, then finger-combed the front of her hair.

For the first time I noticed a small gift bag on the bed with a bold "V" printed in calligraphy.

"Should I open this now?" I asked Trace and headed towards the bed.

"That's not from me," he said, positioning both of our pieces of luggage against the wall.

"That's from me," my mom said. "And it shouldn't be a surprise what's in there."

I stuck my hand in the bag and snatched out a pair of yellow fluffy socks, with bright red apples.

"Get it. The apples? New York."

"Yes, mom. They're perfect."

"I knew you would," she boasted. My mom held onto Jazzy P's arm. "I have my man. Now you get yours."

"Gladly," I said.

Chapter 20

The next chapter of life…

Trace and I stood in the middle of Times Square, my fingers looped through the straps of the black stilettos I'd worn to the Broadway show. With my foldable flats snug around my feet, I was only a couple of inches shorter than him. No one seemed to mind that we were blocking the flow of traffic. We weren't the only ones having a moment. There was a toddler having a meltdown over a dropped scoop of strawberry ice cream and a group of teenagers in matching black leotards taking selfies while doing gymnastic tricks. They'd attracted a crowd.

But I think we had attracted angels, because I swear I could hear them singing over my heads.

"Everything about today has been perfect. I wish it didn't have to end so soon."

"Me either," Trace said. "I wanted to give you an unforgettable day. I hope I did."

"You did," I said. "And wait until my blog fans read this. You're going to be the most longed for mystery man in history."

"I only want for one woman to long for me," Trace said.

"And I think she probably does," I said. I shivered and without a second thought Trace slipped off his suit jacket and draped it over my shoulders. A couple walked past that reminded me of my mother and Jazzy P, only twenty years from now. After the outstanding performance of The Lion King, they'd scampered off in the opposite direction from us, hypnotized by the big city and bright lights. I doubted I'd hear from them until morning.

"If I've counted right, then I owe you one more date to complete your Mix and Mingle. Horseback riding, lunch, The Lion King. It's going to be hard to top this one."

"I'm sure you'll come up with something," I said, fanning away the confetti that some unknown source had thrown in the air. It sprinkled down on us like glittery rain, pieces of it sticking to the shoulders of Trace's shirt.

I pinched off one. "They're hearts," I grinned.

Trace blew softly in my face and brushed off the heart-shaped confetti that had stuck to my cheeks.

"Do you want another reason?" Trace said.

"Give me a reason."

"Because even the heavens know we're in love, Vaughn."

He kissed me. I kissed him. We kissed each other. That was reason enough for me.

Enjoy Other Books by Tia McCollors

Fiction
A Heart of Devotion
Zora's Cry
The Truth About Love
The Last Woman Standing
Steppin' Into The Good Life
Friday Night Love
Sunday Morning Song
Monday Morning Joy
Christmas Angels (A Short Story)

Non-Fiction
If These Shoes Could Talk
(Prissy Purse Devotions)

About The Author

TIA MCCOLLORS is an award-winning, bestselling author and speaker. Since the success of her first novel, A Heart of Devotion (2005), Tia has continually nurtured her writing career. She is the author of a growing number of inspirational romance and women's fiction titles. Tia has also become well-known as a significant and fresh voice for Christian devotionals.

Tia's most recent works include The Days of Grace series that includes **Friday Night Love, Sunday Morning Song,** and the August 2015 upcoming release, **Monday Morning Joy.**

Website: www.TiaMcCollors.com
Connect with Tia on
Facebook: www.Facebook.com/FansofTia
Twitter: @TiaMcCollors

Made in the USA
San Bernardino, CA
30 July 2015